A Lightbulb's Lament

By Grant Wamack

(Rare/Based Edition)

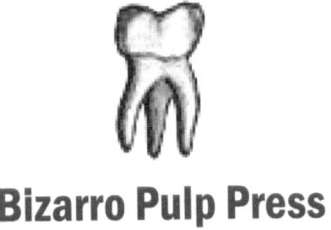

Bizarro Pulp Press

Bizarro Pulp Press

www.BIZARROPULPPRESS.com

A Lightbulb's Lament
Copyright © 2014 Grant Wamack

ISBN-10: 0692227539
ISBN-13: 978-0692227534

Printed in the USA.

Interior image by Grant Wamack and Brandon Duncan

Interior layout by Lori Michelle
www.theauthorsalley.com

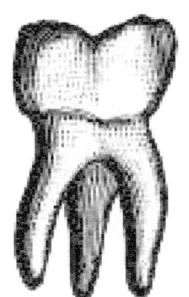

Dedicated to Miss Kerrigan.
I didn't forget that promise.

Acknowledgements

I want to thank Kevin L. Donihe for working with me on the first couple of drafts, Jordan Krall for the constant support and encouragement, Vincenzo Bilof for pushing me, Kris Saknussemm for helping me keep my head screwed on right, Bizarro Pulp Press for giving my baby a home, the bizarro community and shout-out to all the depressed people. This one's for you.

1.

Click.
A light emerged from the darkness like a great flame.

Mr. Watts woke in a daze, absently feeling the curves of his glass head. He stretched his limbs and they cracked like old weathered bones.

He dusted off his cream-colored suit and wiped thick cobwebs off his black dress shoes that were in desperate need of a shine, and a flurry of insects scuttled behind a pile of petrified timber. He considered going back to sleep, easing into that warm electric darkness buzzing beneath his eyelids, but he couldn't let the day go to waste. It would be unbecoming of a gentleman.

Surveying the small space constructed of faded pine wood, Mr. Watts noticed rusty shovels hanging from long nails, a chainsaw with chipped teeth and images of scantily-clad women lining the grungy walls.

Where am I? he wondered. He strained to remember how he arrived here, tracing the illusive curves of the question hanging in his mind, but failed to recall a single shred of evidence pointing him in the right direction.

Someone jiggled the doorknob from outside; Mr. Watts was unsure if he should allow the stranger inside. The polite side of him felt compelled to open the door, but the other side harbored a deep fear of whatever stood outside.

The stranger banged on the door repeatedly and the weak frame shook violently. Mr. Watts cringed with each booming knock and the power reverberated throughout the shed and knocked dust into the air.

Mr. Watts swallowed a thick cloud of dust mites, dead skin cells, and bits of soil. He doubled over into a coughing fit, held his gut and sneezed.

"H-hold on one second . . . I'm coming. One minute." His throat was dry and raspy. Cold breath floated in the claustrophobic space like a ghost straining to embrace something firm, something solid.

Clutching his chest, Mr. Watts opened the door and watched his breath fade into nothingness. A bone-numbing breeze drifted inside and he staggered backward. He wrapped his arms around his chest and shivered uncontrollably.

A short naked man with stubby fingers and a thick layer of grey hairs stood before him totally unaware of the sub-zero temperature. He observed the disgusted look on Mr. Watts's curved face and inspected his immaculate suit. Thoroughly shaken, he retreated and fled into the dark haze.

Mr. Watts was thrown off by the naked man's reaction, but quickly regained his composure and shouted as loud as he could muster, which wasn't very loud at all.

"Sir! Please don't run. Perhaps we can find suitable clothing for you."

The naked man was long gone, swallowed by the all-encompassing darkness. All that remained of his existence were a few grey hairs scattered on the doorstep.

Mr. Watts stood there—fingers growing numb—and contemplated his next move. He stuffed his hands into his pockets and ran into the cold. Despite his best intentions, the sheer amount of snow slowed him down. He was up to his ankles in glittering white and he was surrounded by a thick, cloying darkness.

Wings of sorrow fluttered in his chest. Heartbeat fluttering. Fluttering like sad wings. Sorrowful wings.

Wings that didn't know where to go or why they were flapping at all, but just going through the motions. His heartbeat fluttered and he didn't know why.

With a heavy sigh, he continued trudging forward through the tundra. The bottom of his pant legs were becoming wet and his thin socks did little to protect his feet from the chill.

Mr. Watts stopped in his tracks and shuddered as a primal roar swelled out of the darkness. There was a brief hush and the soft patter of snow hitting the ground. A blood-curdling scream gradually rose out of the silence, climbing a ladder of unnatural octaves and reaching its crescendo before being cut off.

Running at full speed, Mr. Watts couldn't see but eight feet ahead of him—an endless stretch of night.

Just when he thought he was going to pass out from lack of oxygen and a bad exercising regimen, he caught sight of two figures wrestling on the perimeter of his light.

One was huge; an overbearing figure who was in desperate need of a bath, and the other loosely resembled a small child. Still, Mr. Watts crept closer;

nerves on edge, he realized it was not a child. In fact, it was the naked man from earlier and he was losing a massive amount of blood.

Mr. Watts wanted to intervene and make things right, but he knew he knew he didn't stand a chance. He cringed as he watched from a safe distance, eyes fixated on the horrific spectacle unfolding before him—a cold origami effigy of death bursting with sharp angles and teeth.

He was frozen in place, an icy spectator living out his last days.

The resounding snap of the naked man's spine shook Mr. Watts out of his hypnotic state, yet a cold knot remained lodged in his chest.

The giant sloth lumbered toward Mr. Watts's radius of light, swinging its long arms; a red splash of blood stained its mangy brown fur. The naked man hung out of its ragged mouth like a cheap toothpick. The sloth wolfed down its prey and burped.

Disgusted by the sloth's utter lack of table manners and ruthless killing methods, Mr. Watts searched his pockets for his well-read copy of *Miss Kerrigan's Essential Guide to Manners 3rd Edition,* but he seemed to have misplaced it.

The giant sloth appraised Mr. Watts with its black beady eyes and licked its thin lips. Fat drops of saliva sprinkled the ground—melting snow wherever they fell—revealing patches of long-dead crabgrass.

Mr. Watts didn't like it. As a matter of fact, he didn't like it one bit. "Please keep your eyes to yourself, sir. Staring is unkind and unwholesome, and don't get me started on your table manners. Lumbering around as a beast is not a suitable excuse for your actions today."

The sloth backed up and grunted—offended by the remark. Cheeks red with embarrassment, the sloth licked excess blood off its sharp claws and ran off on all fours.

"And good day to you too," Mr. Watts muttered.

2.

Mr. Watts's teeth chattered as he walked through the snow and darkness, cold and alone. It was bad enough that it had to be completely dark and freezing; snow began to drift down from the chiaroscuro sky in thick flakes, glittering in his circle of light.

Snowflakes peppered the back of Mr. Watts's pear-shaped head. Each flake made a *ppfff* sound the moment it touched his warmth and rose in smoky tendrils.

It became irritating, yet he resigned himself to his harsh surroundings and focused on walking forward with his head down.

Through the grainy landscape, Mr. Watts managed to spot the dim outline of buildings in the distance. Hope swam inside his gut. *Perhaps I'll run into someone with some manners*, he thought.

Something crashed into the small of his back and he stumbled forward, crying out in pain. He turned around and looked down at the woman lying down in the snow rubbing her elbow.

She was a stunning brunette sporting a rose gold septum nose ring and a thick brown coat comprised of a variety of animal fur draped over her shoulders. She huffed and puffed, staring in awe at the man with the lightbulb head standing over her.

"Stop staring and help me up," the brunette said, brushing the snow off her coat.

Mr. Watts rushed over, grabbed her hand and helped her to her feet.

The woman shot a nervous glance over her shoulder and turned back to the man, wondering if she could trust him. He seemed innocent enough. "Who are you? And what's with the lightbulb?"

"I-I apologize. That was wrong of me." He gently took hold of the brunette's soft hand and kissed her knuckle. "My name is Mr. Watts. It's a pleasure to meet you and I'm not sure what you mean. Is there something wrong with my head?"

"No. It's just you stick out like a sore thumb. I've never seen anyone like you. My name's Prisma by the way."

Mr. Watts's lightbulb turned a light blue as he felt the heavy weight of depression settle into his thoughts. "Nice to meet you Prisma. Perhaps I should be on my way . . . "

Mr. Watts felt exposed not only to the cold weather, but his insides; the ugly parts were stripped clean, laid bare to this strange woman. He wanted to leave. Be anywhere but here.

"No, wait . . . you should stick around a little bit." Prisma shifted her stance, leaning her weight on her right side. "It's nice to see a fresh face. Seeing the same people day after day becomes monotonous and draining—you know. Feels like I'm stuck in a time loop." She laughed.

Her cheery laughter filled Mr. Watts with new-found warmth and his lightbulb head's color shifted, turning a hot pink. "What's so funny?"

"Well your outfit and your head are kind of weird. You don't even have a face."

Mr. Watts felt crushed by the weight of her words, even though he knew she was right. No one he had seen so far possessed any type of electrical appliance for a head. All he'd seen was flesh, bone and cartilage. He *felt* like he had a mouth, eyes, nose. But when his hands move over the lightbulb that was his head, there was nothing.

Prisma placed her warm hand on his shoulder and gave it a small squeeze. "Look, I'm sorry. I didn't mean to hurt your feelings, but someone much worse than me could've found you. If it's any consolation, you're a very well-dressed gentleman and that tie is über cute."

Mr. Watts smoothed the wrinkles out of his tie, held his head up high, and beamed a marigold yellow. "Thank you. Much appreciated."

"No biggie. You know I could use your help?"

"How may I be of service?"

"I'm kind of on the run from some bad people and I'm lost. I know I'm close to home, but it seems to be darker than usual and . . . "

"Of course. A gentleman always helps a lady in need." Mr. Watts puffed his chest out.

"Great. You can come over for a bit and get out of the cold. Have a drink or something to eat. I'm sure you're starving."

Mr. Watts's stomach grumbled and he couldn't remember the last time he ate. "I would love to but I don't want to be a burden."

"No, no—it would be fine. You could meet the Doc while you're at it."

"I suppose I can stop by, since you insist. May I ask who the Doc is?" Mr. Watts pictured a mean old man with gigantic spectacles, disheveled hair and an appalling wardrobe. He trembled in fear at the possibility of meeting this intimidating, uncouth man.

Prisma's violet eyes sparkled as they reflected his warm light. She grabbed his hand firmly and moved her black bangs out of her eyes. "Shut up and follow me."

Prisma guided Mr. Watts through a labyrinth of run-down buildings, crumbling warehouses, and long-abandoned factories. The pungent air of desolation pervaded the small town like an unwelcome guest.

Mr. Watts wondered what this locale looked like in the past. He imagined a clean, bustling town full of sunlight and happy faces. However, at some undetermined point in time something tragic occurred which broke the heart of the town—shattering each fragile chamber into a fine dust. And a town with no heart might as well be nothing but a ghost in a shell.

Mr. Watts let out a heavy sigh.

"What are you sighing about?" Prisma asked.

"Oh, nothing. Just thinking about the past."

She tapped his head. "Well don't overthink it.'Kay?"

Mr. Watts glanced at a torched bungalow to his right—an architect's nightmare. It was covered head to toe in broken clocks, smashed time faces, and a few awkwardly placed windows. He thought it may have been a trick of the light reflecting off the snow, but a doughy pale face pressed itself flush against the window's grimy surface.

"Hey Prisma, whatever is that young child doing up there?"

He gestured back to the window, now empty and dark. There were no signs whatsoever of a child being there. It might as well have been nothing, just his imagination running wild.

"Oh don't worry. Those snot-nosed brats are always running around. Completely reckless if you ask me. Be careful around them. They're some sneaky bastards."

Mr. Watts was taken aback by Prisma's sharp words. He blinked his eyes over and over, making sure this was the same sweet, polite woman he met earlier and not a doppleganger.

"Prisma, please watch your language. Ladies of your caliber shouldn't speak such obscenities."

Prisma waved him off. "Mr. Watts, I'm just speaking my mind . . . this isn't the 1950's where women slave over the oven and cater to men. Stop being old-fashioned."

The air rushed out of Mr. Watts's lungs and he struggled to breathe. It might as well have been the equivalent of a prize fighter delivering a swift jab to the ribs. "You think I'm old-fashioned?"

"Well—yeah."

Mr. Watts grew silent and incredibly self-conscious. *Am I really old-fashioned?* he thought, and began the slow tedious process of sifting through everything he had ever said in life. It was difficult to remember . . .

"Okay, we're here. Wait outside; I'm going to talk to Doc for a second and make sure everything's all right. Okay?"

Mr. Watts nodded. "Okay, but what am I supposed to do in your absence?"

Prisma moved a strand of jet black hair out of her eyes and smiled. "Just wait here patiently. Don't be nervous. I'll be out in a jiffy. Promise."

Mr. Watts nodded. He wasn't quite sure how long

a jiffy entailed, but he was sure he could wait that length of time. He was a man of great patience—or at least he thought so.

In the meantime, Mr. Watts observed Prisma's home. It was a mid-sized house compared to the other incredibly small homes which lined the block. The only difference was this one seemed to be in much better shape. There were chunks of red brick missing from the walls and holes in the tinfoil roof, but besides that it was a solid structure.

Mr. Watts leaned against the house and stared into the darkness while he patiently waited. After a few minutes passed, his back began to ache from leaning for too long, and he got the strange feeling that he was being watched.

Something scuffled nearby, kicking up snow in its wake.

Mr. Watts feared for his life. "Who's out there?" his voice cracked.

The wind howled like a banshee.

"I repeat, who's out there? Show yourself now o-or else."

Silence.

Mr. Watts wished Prisma had never left him out here, vulnerable to the elements and who knows what else. He kept glancing at the door and back to the darkness, expecting Prisma to come outside any moment. But that moment wouldn't come no matter how hard he stared at the door.

Something whizzed through the darkness and narrowly missed Mr. Watts's head by mere inches. He touched the metal ridges spiraling down the base of his neck just to reassure himself his head hadn't become unscrewed.

Mr. Watts took a deep breath and steeled himself for any more mysterious objects aimed at his head. He would be ready this time, prepared for the worst.

A pale boy, wearing loosely-knitted clothes too big for his small frame, ran out of the darkness, pummeling Mr. Watts with a barrage of snowballs. He laughed wildly like demon spawn.

Mr. Watts backpedaled and threw his hands up—shielding his puffy face. Just when he regained his balance he slipped on a patch of ice and fell—crying out in horror. Even though his head was still reeling from the assault, he managed to feel around blindly, groping handfuls of snow and air until his hand closed around a hefty chunk of ice. He wiped the snow out of his eyes and picked the chunk up and threw it with all his might.

It cut through the darkness—whistling—and something shattered. It sounded strangely like glass falling softly on the snow. *Perhaps it was a window*, Mr. Watts thought.

It was way too dark for him to see, but he sensed something was terribly wrong. "Excuse me, are you okay?"

Silence.

A batch of butterflies flew out of the darkness—an upstream rainbow of cascading colors briefly wrapped around Mr. Watt's dome before flying away.

He watched in awe as they disappeared.

Mr. Watts wondered where the boy went. No way he could have gotten away so quickly. He walked into the darkness apprehensively, sure the kid was waiting to attack him with more snowballs. He stepped down on something hard yet fragile, smashing it to bits. He looked down and saw a multitude of cracked porcelain pieces. Then he realized with horror these weren't pieces of porcelain—they had belonged to the boy. The rest of his body was scattered nearby.

A gust of wind picked up the smallest pieces and carried them away.

Mr. Watts felt a terrible guilt grip his body. He trembled and wept in the sudden realization of what he had done—murder.

Murder.

"Mr. Watts! Why are you crying?" Prisma asked.

Embarrassed, Mr. Watts wiped away his tears and sniffled. "I wasn't crying . . . there was something in my eye. Dust or something of that matter."

"Oh . . . I see." Prisma noticed the boy's shattered remains decorating the snow. "Don't worry Mr. Watts, everything's okay. Children get killed all the time. It's normal. And in all actuality, they're better off dead."

"Do you truly mean that?"

"Yes. Really. Now get up and come inside. We can have something to eat. That'll make you feel better."

"I suppose you're right."

Prisma grabbed his warm, sweaty hand and clasped it inside her own. She led him back to her house and opened the door. It was humid and dim inside.

Candles sat atop every shelf and ledge, throwing monstrous shadows on the walls. A mixture of sweet and pungent aromas swept through every inch of the house.

A silhouette sitting in a tattered crimson recliner shifted its weight. A man stood up and revealed himself. He was rail-thin with a grey receding hairline, a lab coat a couple sizes too big; liver spots dotted his forehead and a nice set of frames sat on the bridge of his sharp nose.

"Hi, I'm Doctor Reynolds, or you can call me Doc. Nice to meet you." He stuck his right hand out and adjusted his gold-rimmed glasses with his left.

Mr. Watts shook his hand firmly and a slight tingling sensation ran through his forearm—an electrical current of sorts. "It's a pleasure. I'm Mr. Watts."

"That's what I've been told. You seem like an interesting fellow. Very light-hearted I assume." Doctor Reynolds grinned. "Excuse the terrible pun."

Mr. Watts chuckled. "Don't mind me. I love puns. Actually, wordplay of any kind, to be honest."

"That's good. I'm starting to like this guy, Prisma."

"I knew you would." She took off her coat and hung it up on a coat rack made of elk antlers.

"Would you like something to eat?"

"Yes, as long as it's no trouble."

Prisma walked into the kitchen, moving about the tight space like a beautiful pale ghost. She returned with a thick blueberry muffin and a cup of some indistinct liquid.

He grabbed it and thanked her before devouring the muffin in one solid bite and downing the cold—yet strangely satisfying—drink.

Both Doctor Reynolds and Prisma stared in disbelief. The food disappeared into the lightbulb, even though Mr. Watts believed he was opening a mouth he didn't actually have and shoving the food down his throat.

Mr. Watts blushed as he noticed their stares and gaping mouths. "Excuse me. I guess I was a little hungry."

"You act like you haven't eaten in ages," Prisma said.

"Well I've been asleep for quite some time and my memory's a little hazy." He carefully wiped his mouth with a napkin.

"Don't want to sound intrusive, but do you have any idea where you came from? Any recollection whatsoever of your past?" Doctor Reynolds asked.

"No, as a matter of fact all I pull up is a blank. I know there's something there but . . . "

"You're like a newborn." Prisma jumped up and down, clapping her hands.

"Prisma, relax. It's okay Mr. Watts—these things happen. Everything should come back in due time."

"I hope you're right."

"These things usually work themselves out. But it's getting late. Please excuse me, a man my age needs his rest. Good night."

Doctor Reynolds disappeared into a dark room down the hall.

"How can he tell when it's night and day? It's always dark."

"Circadian rhythm. The clock that never stops."

"Well, I guess I should be getting on my way."

Prisma's face flushed with worry. "No . . . where will you stay?"

"I don't know, but I'm sure I'll be able to find a place if I look hard enough."

"I'm not so sure about that. You can stay the night."

"Really? I don't want to be any trouble."

"No, not all. It would be . . . an honor. We haven't had a guest in so long."

Mr. Watts beamed. "Well, thank you kindly the invitation. I suppose I could stay for just one night."

"Good. I'll grab you a spare pillow and some blankets. You can sleep on the couch. It's much more comfortable than it looks."

Prisma hurried off into a dark room. After some loud rummaging, she ran back out with her hands full of colorful blankets and a fluffy pillow.

Mr. Watts helped Prisma lay the blankets on the couch and their hands briefly brushed against one another. They both blushed.

"Once again, thank you very much. I am much obliged."

"You too. I'll be right down the hall. Don't be afraid to help yourself to anything. *Mi casa, su casa.*"

Mr. Watts nodded. He watched Prisma glide down the hall into her room and shut the door.

Her scent lingered like azaleas floating on ice. He snuggled beneath the blankets—comforted by the smell—and let the darkness settle over his eyes.

3.

Mr. Watts was a cute little boy with a lightbulb head slightly too big for his small gangly frame and a miniature suit—the first of many.

He watched the other kids run around the courtyard; a gang of screaming rascals. They threw balls at each other and a few kicked them to kingdom come. Some kids preferred to just run around in circles, chasing infinity.

A dirty blue kickball rolled over to where Mr. Watts sat in the grass. He placed his book about etiquette beside him, but made sure his page was bookmarked before doing so.

A chubby kid with freckles, a shock of red hair, and a big nose ran toward him—full steam.

Mr. Watts stood, inspected his suit for any grass or dirt, and handed him the ball.

Big nose snatched the ball out of his hand, shoved Mr. Watts, and ran away. "Thanks, pussy."

Mr. Watts walked home with his head hung lower than usual and tossed his book bag on the living room table.

His father noticed Mr. Watts's bruised face and his jaw dropped. "What the hell happened to your face?"

"A kid shoved me."

"That's no good. I hate bullies. Son, you can't let people run all over you. You have to stand up for yourself and you don't always have to do it with your fists."

Mr. Watts nodded.

The next day, Mr. Watts saw the big-nosed boy bouncing his blue ball.

"Hey, what the hell are you looking at? Why don't you go have a tea party, faggot?"

"First off, I'm not a faggot. A faggot is a bundle of sticks. Secondly, you should invest in a dictionary, big nose."

The big-nosed bully's face crumpled up like a page of loose leaf paper and gave way to tears. "My nose isn't that big, is it?" He felt every inch of his nose, trying to get an accurate feel for how large his nose was and if it exceeded the set dimensions he harbored in his mind.

Mr. Watts nodded.

Big nose wiped the stream of mucus from his nose and ran off, leaving his ball behind.

Mr. Watts smiled.

4.

Mr. Watts rolled over and woke up with a start. He wiped the sweat off his glass head and rose from the tattered couch on shaky legs.

"I should really watch what I eat," he muttered.

A blood-curdling scream echoed throughout the house.

Prisma!

Mr. Watts ran toward Prisma's room. He tripped over something bulky and fell—landing on his shoulder. He painfully lifted himself from the floor and almost screamed with abysmal horror when he noticed Doctor Reynolds's limp body beneath him.

"Doctor Reynolds! Doctor Reynolds, are you all right?"

No response.

Mr. Watts grabbed him by the shoulders and shook him. "Doctor Reynolds, what on earth is going on?"

Doctor Reynolds's foggy eyes flickered open for a moment and he mumbled, "Prisma . . . help her," before slipping back into unconsciousness.

Mr. Watts charged into her room and saw two silhouettes fighting in the darkness. He strode further inside and his presence illuminated the conflict in a dazzling light.

It looked like a tornado had spun through the room. A smashed window, an antiquated dresser lay on its side—drawers open like steps, clothes strewn everywhere. And in the middle of this shadowy destruction, Prisma struggled to keep an obese woman at bay.

The obese woman in question resembled a well-fed bull; she wrapped her hamhock arms around Prisma's small waist. Prisma whipped her head from side to side, attempting to shimmy her thin arms out of the obese woman's grip. The obese woman spied Mr. Watts standing in the doorway, shied away from the vibrant light, and hissed.

A thick writhing vein in the obese woman's neck bulged, threatening to burst. Prisma's purple eyes grew dull and glossy and she fell limp.

The obese woman slung Prisma over her broad shoulders and smashed the window with her thick fist. A gale of cold wind infiltrated the room and the obese woman puckered her lips and blew Mr. Watts a sickening kiss before leaping into the cold snow.

Cursing his lack of heroism, Mr. Watts watched helplessly as Prisma was taken away into the darkness. A shroud of sorrow settled over him and the cold crept inside like an anaconda, slithering into the creases and folds of his suit, working its way toward his beating heart.

5.

After an indeterminable amount of time, Mr. Watts forced himself out of his state of lament. *There's no time for this*, he thought, *I have to save Prisma by any means*.

He walked into the hall, found Doctor Reynolds, and smacked him five times before he finally woke up.

"Wah? Wah?" Were the only two words Doctor Reynolds could spit out.

"Doctor Reynolds, we need to find Prisma. A rather fat lady choked her into submission and kidnapped her."

Doctor Reynolds squinted at the man with the lightbulb for a head and a cold realization set in. "Oh no! Must be one of the Gutter Bitches."

"Gutter Bitches?"

"They're terrible, ill-mannered women who could lose more than a few pounds. Prisma used to work for them."

"Well that one was rather unseemly. What are we going to do?"

"Unseemly is an understatement but I'm afraid I can't do anything. I'm too old and the day has already taken a toll on my heart. Any more tragedy might kill me."

"So I—"

"—Yes, you have to go out there and save Prisma. Please do so and I will forever be in your debt."

Mr. Watts looked at the crumpled old man before him, rolled his neck, and took a deep breath.

"I'll do it."

It's what a gentleman would do.

6.

Mr. Watts hesitantly stepped out into the cold darkness and wrapped a long black scarf around his neck. He valiantly walked forward with Doctor Reynolds's directions mapped out in his mind.

For a moment, he swelled up with absolute hopelessness. *How am I supposed to find the Gutter Bitches in this sea of darkness? No landmarks, barely any guidance . . .*

He reared his head up and trod forward, ready to defy the odds. Finally, after what seemed like an eternity, he found exactly what he was searching for—the Gutter Bitch abode.

It wasn't exactly hard to miss, even with snow coming down in thick, blinding flakes. Bass-heavy music poured out from the darkness—flooding the air—leading Mr. Watts directly to his destination.

The building resembled a massive banana wrapped in tinfoil. The immense structure swayed from side to side, vibrating violently.

As Mr. Watts approached, his whole body began to shake and his glass head vibrated more violently than the building itself. He fingered a small hairline fracture at the base of his neck and worried about his safety, questioning his motives and his sanity.

7.

Mr. Watts took his scarf off his neck and wrapped it around his entire head, covering every inch of his bulb except for a thin slit for his eyes. He grabbed hold of the slick door handle and his entire arm thrummed with a heavy vibration emanating from inside. He opened the door and was slapped by a barrage of hand claps, kick drums, and an irritatingly loud bass system that made his ears ring.

The dance floor was slick with booze, cigarette butts, heavy feet covered in combat boots, and big women with gaudy piercings. Some sported multicolored Mohawks, black leather jackets, and denim jeans, while others wore clothes way too tight for their plump bodies. A group of Gutter Bitches by the door pumped their fists and ignored Mr. Watts as he stepped inside.

The club was dark, punctuated by thin green crystals jutting out from spongy walls that gave the Gutter Bitches a sickly pallor as they passed by its light.

Two of them—quite possibly a couple—jumped up and down, producing mini tremors that ran through the floor and almost threw Mr. Watts off his feet.

Mr. Watts was slammed by visions of his impending death as he struggled to steady himself in the sea of bodies. The first showcased him being smashed in between a fatal collision of fat flesh, crushing his thin body into a soft bloody pulp. Another showed him being pulled apart like a piece of chicken, his arms snapping off and one woman—a rather gluttonous victor—waved around his femur like a trophy.

He shook off these visions and remembered why he was here in the first place: Prisma. He quickly closed the door behind him and tried his best to maneuver through the sweat-drenched bodies and pounding music without causing any trouble. He had no idea where to go but he successfully squeezed by two Gutter Bitches without being noticed or squished in the process.

A trio of Gutter Bitches, each sporting exotic slut stamps on their lower backs, shared a bottle of aged sloth tonic. The foul liquid trickled down one bitch's double chin and disappeared into her cleavage. She wiped it off with the back of her hand and ran it through her ocean blue mohawk and laid her electric blue eyes on Mr. Watts, batting her thick eyelashes and shaking her hippo hips.

Her eyes sparkled with joy and excitement and something else—lust.

She glided over to him, attracted by the light spilling out from the cracks of his scarf. She bent over, hands touching the dirty ground, and twerked her huge ass for Mr. Watts.

Her pants began to slip down her pudgy waist and her pink thong began to show. Mr. Watts tried to look away, but he was mesmerized by the horrible gyrations. Then her body odor, which smelled like wet dog and cottage cheese, penetrated his nostrils.

Mr. Watts doubled over and vomited the little food he had left in his stomach. He slipped into a pocket of darkness to recover and get a hold of his bearings.

The image of those two enormous moons—jiggling like planets out of orbit—haunted the outskirts of his mind. He thought he spied a small village of crustaceans on her behind, living in squalor. He wished it was a hallucination, but he knew better.

Bordering on sensory overload, Mr. Watts was overcome by the sudden need to get out and catch a breath of fresh air, even if that meant going back outside. Anything was better than this.

Prisma's beautiful face rose in his mind, hovering briefly before mouthing his name. *Mr. Watts, Mr. Watts* . . . Her face grew faint, watercolor soft, and faded away.

He had to find her. It was his duty as a gentleman.

Mr. Watts sidled past more fat bodies, finding pockets of elbow room and rank air. The journey felt endless; an infinite amount of fat seemed to get in his way but he finally reached a door. He leaned his head against the cold metal and rested on the door for support. "Thank you," he whispered to himself.

Two female voices argued behind the door-one sweet and the other coarse. Mr. Watts snapped to attention. He ignored the blaring music and focused on the voices. He tuned in until he could hear every word.

"Shut the fuck up bitch!"

" . . . I'm done with that life. *Finito*. I thought I made that clear. I want to do something better than this."

"It doesn't matter what you want. Don't you see that? I'm running a goddamn business here! I had a fuckin' guy come in the other day asking for you and he was willing to provide us with some vintage sloth tonic and rare animal skins. But nooooo, Miss Prisma thinks she's too booshy for the business."

Mr. Watts gasped when he heard Prisma's name.

"Well I'll tell you something. You're going to put out if you like it or not—you little dirty whore. Forget your dreams of making an honest living, and forget about a singing career. I want to meet the guy who told you that lie." There was a loud crash and someone yelled out in pain.

Mr. Watts took a breath and kicked the door. He kicked it again, giving it more *umph,* and it surrendered. Shards of wood and splinter flew like darts, sticking in the yellowed walls.

In the middle of the room there was a large, pink Victorian-style bed fit for a queen. And on top of the bed lay Prisma. She was reflected ten times over in the mirrors covering the walls and ceiling.

Prisma froze in place, half-naked. Her scratched shoulder poked through the tattered remains of her shirt and her small tits nearly spilled out her ripped bra. Rorschach bruises flowered on her still-pretty face. But the thing that surprised Mr. Watts the most was the gleaming patches of machinery whirring and puffing smoke inside her exposed stomach.

A single tear ran down her face.

Mr. Watts shook with anger, an uncontrollable rage. Rage at the Gutter Bitches, rage at the cold churning inside his bones, rage at the utter lack of human decency and respect. He shook violently and his light transitioned from bright yellow to a red, pulsating glow.

The Gutter Bitch was beyond huge. Her fat spilled

out of her polka-dotted lingerie in rolls and her panties were a few sizes too small.

"Fuck are you doing here, freak?"

Dipping her head down, the Gutter Bitch charged Mr. Watts like a linebacker from Hell.

Prisma slipped under the bed, dripping large drops of blood behind her, soaking into the cigarette-stained carpet.

Mr. Watts's lightbulb turned a deep, raging red and a circle of light sliced through the air like an oscillating blade.

The Gutter Bitch slumped over, cut in half by raw electromagnetic energy. Her top half toppled to the floor and blood geysered from her lower half, spraying the ceiling a vibrant red.

The damaged canopy hanging over the bed was smothered in tomato red and tilted over the side of the headboard.

Sprawled on the ground, Mr. Watts tried to get a handle on his raging headache. He massaged his head softly until the throbbing pain eased away and the residual pressure dissipated. He felt spent and utterly devoid of energy.

Prisma crawled out from underneath the bed on hands and knees. Her puffy red eyes lit up once she saw Mr. Watts was safe. She got up and ambled over to where he was sitting. She crouched down and hugged him tightly.

Mr. Watts managed to hug her back, reveling in her lemon freshness, but pushed her away as he coughed up a bit of blood.

"Are you okay?"

"I hurt all over . . . in places I never knew existed, but I'll be fine. Are you okay?"

"Oh, I'm fine enough. Just a few cuts and bruises. I'm sure they look a lot worse than they really are." She shrugged. "We should probably get going. Who knows what you started."

Prisma grabbed Mr. Watts's hand and helped him to his feet.

"Who was that lady?"

"Used to be one of my old . . . bosses, and she is not a lady. She's a cold-hearted bitch. Good thing you killed her." She spit venomously and the glob landed in the Gutter Bitch's left eye.

"But why did she hurt you? Why would anybody hurt you?"

Prisma laughed. "You're so innocent, Mr. Watts. Some people don't get what they want in this world so they try dragging you and everyone else down into the muck, making life miserable. And to be frank, I wasn't going back to my old life. No way, no how."

Mr. Watts nodded.

"Let's go. Don't want to hang around any longer. Nothing but bad memories here."

They walked into the lobby and were assaulted by the terrible stench of decay and sweat. Gutter Bitches lay slumped over one another like fleshy beanbags and blood filled the cracks in the tiled floor.

The silence was disconcerting.

"Oh my God!!" Prisma pursed her lips.

Mr. Watts looked down at the carnage he created and cringed as he stepped over numerous bodies, some still twitching in their final death throes. They were once alive, and now they lay still—scattered about like grotesque mannequins—caricatures of a distant past.

Prisma bit her bottom lip and Mr. Watts

swallowed hard; they made their way as quickly as they could through the double doors.

8.

Prisma ran through the snow, gripping Mr. Watts's hand. They were alone except for the sound of the snow crunching under their feet and their ragged breaths.

"Why are . . . we running . . . so fast?" Mr. Watts was barely able to spit out these words between labored breaths.

Prisma looked back at him and furrowed her eyebrows.

"We're being followed."

Mr. Watts looked behind him and all he could see was snow, and beyond that darkness and more darkness.

Pumping his weary arms and legs, Mr. Watts picked up the pace. His lungs were on fire, but he fought through the searing pain. Soon enough the house popped up and Mr. Watts's second wind kicked in.

Prisma rushed through the door. It slammed against the wall, creating a large dent. Pieces of drywall tumbled to the ground.

"Doc! Where the hell are you?"

Prisma yelled and pushed a table over as if the Doc was hiding in plain sight.

The Doc seemed to surface from the shadows, but once he saw Prisma he dropped everything and ran to her side. They hugged, gripping each other hard and firm as if the world would end the moment they let go.

"Are you okay, Prisma? I was beginning to get really worried there for a second. You know you're the only family I have left."

Prisma pushed a stray hair away from her eyes and said, "I know, I know, but Mr. Watts came through and saved the day. Everything's all right. The Gutter Bitches are dead."

"Good riddance," the Doc said. "They never had good taste in music anyway."

Mr. Watts's lightbulb flashed a bright red.

"Oh look, he's blushing," Prisma laughed.

The Doc laughed, walked over and shook Mr. Watts's hand.

"I want to thank you, fine sir, for saving Prisma. You truly are a gentleman. Plus your suit looks immaculate despite all the trouble."

Mr. Watts dusted off his suit and swelled up with pride. "Why thank you, Doc. I appreciate your compliments, and in regards to Prisma, it was my duty as a gentleman to save her."

"You did well." Then the Doc turned his attention back to Prisma. "I want you to lie down so I can heal you. I don't want any of those nasty cuts getting infected."

Prisma nodded and laid on the couch.

The Doc crouched over her and moved his palms just a couple inches above her chest and let his hands hover. He swayed from side to side and moved his veiny hands in wide circular arcs, washing an invisible flat plane.

He closed his eyes and began to hum a calm, soothing melody and spoke a string of foreign syllables under his breath.

Prisma looked calm and serene with her arms across her shoulders. *Coffin ready* was a phrase that flitted across Mr. Watts's mind.

The Doc placed his trembling hands on Prisma's exposed stomach and his body shook. Slight tremors ran through his crooked spine.

Mr. Watts grew worried for the Doc's health. He thought the he was going to fall over any moment now, but he stayed back out of respect and fear.

The Doc's hands quivered and emitted a small canary yellow glow. Fresh strands of smooth skin criss-crossed over the cut in Prisma's shoulder, and it was good as new.

Mr. Watts's jaw dropped and his heart skipped a beat. He wanted to ask a million questions, but he kept his mouth shut and marveled at the magical display.

The Doc's hands shook even harder and sweat beaded on his wrinkled forehead. There was something terribly wrong. The glow dimmed, returned for a moment and faded away completely.

The Doc collapsed, falling to his knees.

"Doc, are you okay?" Mr. Watts asked, moving in to help.

"I-I'll be all right. Just need to take a breath. Healing drains me . . . and now that I'm getting older, it doesn't work as well as it used to."

"You still did good," Prisma said, appraising her smooth, unblemished skin. "For the most part, my cuts and bruises are healed. I feel ten times better."

The Doc smiled weakly and his wrinkled dimples

became prominent. His expression quickly soured. "Do you hear that?"

"Hear what?" Mr. Watts asked.

"Hush. Listen." Prisma cocked her head sideways.

Mr. Watts strained to listen, but heard nothing. He stared questioningly at the Doc and Prisma.

"You hear it, don't you?" Doc asked, waiting for his suspicions to be confirmed.

"Yeah it's barely audible, but definitely there." Prisma confirmed his worst suspicions.

Mr. Watts grew worried and grabbed Prisma's freshly healed shoulder. "Excuse me, I don't want to be a pest, but what exactly are you talking about?"

"*Telemarketers*," she whispered and looked around fearfully.

The room became quiet and an uncomfortable silence made itself known.

The Doc slowly stood. "I think we need to get going. We don't have much time. Gather your things. We're leaving."

Prisma ran into the darkness and began stuffing random clothes and food into a raggedy book bag with patches sewn on the front.

The Doc drank a glass of water and wiped his forehead with a towel. He grabbed a black backpack and moved into the kitchen and stuffed cans of food and kitchen utensils inside until it bulged.

Mr. Watts had nothing except for the clothes on his back so he just watched patiently. To keep his paranoia at bay, he inspected his suit for any lint or specks of dirt. He picked them all off—no matter how minuscule they were.

Finally, the Doc and Prisma finished packing. Primsa was clothed in a large, black and white fur coat which seemed to encompass her whole body except her pale face. The Doc wore a brown leather coat and held a couple of duffle bags in his hands.

"What's in there?" Mr. Watts asked to break the silence.

The Doc grinned. "Just a few things we'll need on the journey."

He threw the smallest bag at Mr. Watts.

Mr. Watts caught the bag, but stumbled backwards and nearly bumped into a small table.

"Let's get out of here. We've already wasted enough time," the Doc said.

They walked outside into the frigid cold, leaving the house behind.

The wind slammed the door shut with a resounding bang.

9.

The trio walked silently for a time, for a long time. Weariness set in. Mr. Watts coughed and watched his smoky breath dissipate into thin air.

"Are you okay?" Primsa asked.

"Yes. Thanks for asking."

There was a beat of silence and the wind howled.

Mr. Watts spoke up. "Where exactly are we going? I feel as if we have been walking for hours."

The Doc adjusted his foggy spectacles. "We're heading down south to see a friend of mine."

"Who's that?" Prisma asked.

"Well, it's an old friend from my days as a professor. I taught experimental medicine and she taught the history of psychic behavior—a popular class. You would be interested to know she's a full-blooded gypsy and very proud of it. She decided to leave the University and go down a different path, and I went my way as well. This was way before the Great Blackout happened."

"Do you think she could possibly help get rid of this Telemarketer?" Prisma asked.

"I certainly hope so. If not, we're most certainly doomed."

"Why's that?" Mr. Watts asked, stricken with fear.

"Telemarketers are dangerous creatures. Once

44

they catch your scent they will follow you till kingdom come. It may take seconds, minutes, or an entire lifetime, but the outcome is always the same—Death."

"But why did they catch my scent as opposed to someone else? I've never even seen a Telemarketer before!" Mr. Watts gripped his head in frustration.

The Doc placed his hands on Mr. Watts's shoulders and stared directly into his lightbulb face. "Relax. These things happen on occasion. No one knows exactly how or why they came about. My best theory is they're an unfortunate bi-product of the darkness. I'm guessing the Telemarketer caught your scent when you saved Prisma."

"You could be right, but I think it might be his light," Prisma said, pulling the coat closer around her shoulders. "It's hard to miss."

"Like a moth to the flame . . . " The Doc said. "Mr. Watts, you saved the only person I care about in this world, and for that I will put my life on the line to get you out of harm's way. I'm not going to lie and say any of us will get by unscathed. But I'm going to try my damnedest to make sure we make it. Just have a little faith. That's all I ask."

Mr. Watts nodded. "Okay. I can do that. I believe in you wholeheartedly, Doc. It's just a little difficult getting adjusted to these . . . developments."

"It's perfectly understandable my boy." Doc smiled and patted Mr. Watts on the back.

The trio continued walking through the deep snow. Every now and then the Doc would pull out a rusty compass and squint at the foggy piece.

The Doc slowed down and shoved his hand in front of Mr. Watts's chest. He stopped and Prisma did the same.

"Hold on a minute. There's something . . . "

Prisma clutched Mr. Watts's shirt collar and trembled.

Click. Click. Click.

"What is that wretched sound?" Mr. Watts's fear doubled when the clicking stopped and was replaced by an eerie silence.

The Doc shot Mr. Watts a dirty look and brought his finger to his thin, chapped lips, shushing Mr. Watts.

Mr. Watts and Prisma both trembled. He couldn't tell if it was from the weather or the mysterious clicking, but he wanted it to stop.

The clicking started up again, a little more hectic now. Click after click after click after click after click after click.

Mr. Watts shut his eyes tight, hoping the clicking would disappear in the darkness behind his eyelids, but it continued nonetheless.

Then, silence.

The Doc looked around, perplexed by the absence of sound.

"Is it over?" Prisma asked.

The Doc surveyed the area with Mr. Watts shining his light, now tinged a jittery purple, and shook his head.

"I believe so, but wouldn't count on it. We need to pick up our pace. I'm not taking any chances."

They picked up their pace, working up a sweat, putting as much distance as they could between them and the clicking.

Mr. Watts looked behind him every few seconds just to make sure nothing was there. He wasn't sure if he could trust his own hearing. He wasn't sure of anything.

Paranoid and tired, they came upon the silhouette of a small town.

"Is this the place?" Prisma asked, hoping deep down it was.

"No," the Doc replied.

"What do you mean, no?" Prisma asked. "Did we take the wrong route? Is your compass fucked?"

"Prisma, why the vulgarity? I'm deeply offended." Mr. Watts's lightbulb turned salmon pink and he looked away.

"Sorry. I'm just stressed," Prisma said, bathed in his light.

"My compass is fine. We need to make a pit stop. Go somewhere full of people. Maybe we can lose Mr. Watts's scent momentarily—might give us some time to rest and rejuvenate."

"Where are we going though?" Mr. Watts asked.

"To the bar."

10.

The majority of buildings populating the small town were nothing more than burnt-out husks, weathered and rusted by the endless snow falling from the charcoal black sky.

White camels stood outside, tethered to steel benches and rusty light poles. They grunted and bayed; they frantically stomped their feet in the snow as if they were begging to be released from their tethers.

Mr. Watts stood clear, fearful of their large bodies, their misshapen humps, and especially their bulbous eyes. He gave them a wide berth.

The Doc led the way inside the old saloon. Thick red candles sat on the center of every table, but barely lit the room enough to see all of its occupants.

Prisma glanced at Mr. Watts with raised eyebrows, wondering why his light was so dim.

Slightly shaken by Prisma's fearful eyes, Mr. Watts held his hands to his face and realized his light wasn't nearly as bright as it usually was. Still, he didn't want to draw attention to himself.

Mr. Watts could feel the searing stares and hear hushed whispers from lonely men. Glasses clinked, people grunted, and chairs slid against the wooden floor. Feeling out of place and antsy, Mr. Watts

48

wanted to turn around and slip back outside, but he held fast and continued walking as if he didn't notice anything wrong.

Pale, scarred faces scowled at him, and misshapen bodies shifted in their chairs, discomforted by his lightbulb head. They didn't have to say a word, might as well have been open books. They thought he was a freak—an anomaly.

He was overcome by deja-vu and a vivid memory poured out of his subconscious.

"Freak, Freak, Freak," his classmates chanted on his first day of high school.

"Calm down, class." The frazzled teacher couldn't help but snicker at her poor student. "Mr. Watts may look a little different, but that doesn't mean we should make him feel bad. We all have our differences. You can take a seat, Mr. Watts."

Mr. Watts sat down and someone threw a crushed ball of paper at his head and laughed. His light turned a rose quartz pink.

"Look! He's turning pink. What a fag," someone in the back said.

Mr. Watts sank down in his seat, wishing he could disappear and his stupid light would go out. He wished the world would go black and swallow everyone in it.

His light turned midnight blue as depression grabbed the reigns of his heart.

"So we could have gone anywhere, but you chose to bring us to a grimy bar?" Prisma shook her head.

"Yes. A bar is perfect," the Doc said. "It's full of people and there are all types of smells. The Telemarketer will lose his mind if he ever comes sniffing around here."

"I sure hope so," said Mr. Watts. Passing by a table, he dragged his finger across the surface and it turned completely black with dirt. "This place is terribly unwholesome."

The Doc laughed and patted Mr. Watts's back. "It'll be okay, Mr. Watts. Just stick close. Wouldn't want the shadows to swallow you up."

Mr. Watts nodded.

Doc found an empty table and sat down. Mr. Watts and Prisma sat on either side of him.

A bald man sporting a dark red bow-tie seemingly came out of nowhere.

"What can I get you guys?"

"Water for the three of us," Prisma said.

"Prisma, why are you being so rude?" Doc asked. "Maybe Mr. Watts wanted something else besides water. Be considerate of others."

"It's okay. Water is fine," said Mr. Watts.

Prisma sulked. "Sorry. I just assumed everyone wanted some water."

Baldhead came back and set down three grimy glasses of water. He looked back to see if he was being watched.

"You guys should probably leave."

"Why?" Prisma said, ready to stand up.

" . . . There's some stuff going down. It's really not a good time to be here. So I suggest you guys finish your water and leave. It would make things easier for everyone."

"Well, we're not going anywhere. We can take care of ourselves. Thank you very much." Prisma sipped her water and crossed her arms.

"Have it your way. I tried to warn you." The bartender walked away.

Mr. Watts's lightbulb shifted colors, changing from a bright yellow to indigo.

"You look worried, Mr. Watts. Please, if you have anything troubling you, by all means tell us," Doc said.

Mr. Watts sighed. "I must admit that I'm concerned. This world is so big and unfamiliar. I feel overwhelmed and I still can't remember a single thing."

"Why do you feel overwhelmed?" Doc adjusted his glasses and shifted his position in his seat.

"I don't know what's going on. How did all this darkness come to pass, and what happened to the sun? I miss it dearly. The light, the warmth . . . "

"A long time ago, there was a blackout. People call it The Great Blackout or The Second Dark Age, but I like the first label personally. No one really knew what happened. The media outlets threw out any answer they could think of. Terrorist attacks, aliens, a modern-day Y2k virus, the Anunnaki coming back to reclaim their land. Others theorized that space junk—an accumulation of dead satellites, spent rockets, and fragment debris from mini collisions—hit a large satellite and caused a domino effect. Consequently, cutting off all forms of electricity on earth."

The Doc paused. He looked exasperated by the explanation, shaken by memories lodged in his words. He gulped down some water and continued on.

"I'm not even sure what happened. A number of things could have caused this, but the point is the whole world lost power and for some reason we were never able to put it back together. There are rumors of rogue scientists attempting to get some power running again, but that's all hearsay."

Prisma chimed in. "How do you think Mr. Watts fits into the scheme of things?"

"It's funny. He seems like some sort of electric messiah that Edison and Tesla would've dreamed up . . ." The Doc scrunched up his face, envious of the feat and thought about his hands and the limited time he had left on this earth. He wished he would've done more in his youth. Cured more people. "But I think it's safe to say he probably was hurt during the initial night of the blackout, slipped into a coma and is now suffering from a mild case of amnesia. Thankfully, you're okay though."

"I don't think I'm—" Mr. Watts tried to say.

Prisma cut him off. "That helped, right?"

"I think so, but I'm still trying to figure out how exactly I got hurt and why I woke up when I did."

A spotlight suddenly appeared from overhead; thousands of fireflies swarmed inside the makeshift lightbulb. It showered the stage in a sickly green light. Tattered curtains parted and revealed a black man; the lower half of his face was covered in thick white scarves.

Prisma pulled her chair closer to the table and clapped excitedly. The Doc straightened up, ready for the show, and Mr. Watts's concerns fell to the wayside.

The patrons went buck wild, alcohol flowing through their veins.

The black man grabbed the wireless microphone off the stand. "It's that time again . . . time for some karaoke!"

Some people went as so far to give a standing ovation. Prisma looked around the room, doe-eyed and excited. She pinched herself to make sure she wasn't imagining this.

"Who's ready to go first?" He scanned the room with his brown eyes.

A skinny man with bug eyes and dirty blond hair ran up to the stage.

"Looks like we have a contender."

The lights dimmed and the black man scrambled offstage, almost tripping over a white Fender guitar.

"This is going to be terrible," said the Doc.

Mr. Watts was too shell-shocked by the Doc's negative opinion to respond. He thought the guy deserved a fair chance, despite his physical appearance. A small part of him empathized with the fellow and wished him luck.

The skinny man on stage opened his mouth and his eyes grew even more bug-eyed. He belted out the first few lines of his alcohol-fueled song and the crowd went wild. People began to fight, drink furiously, and roll around the floor.

Mr. Watts's light intensified as he bobbed his head to the lovely music. It wasn't his usual cup of tea; he preferred classical music and jazz, but there was something soothing about the man's gravel-filled, folksy voice.

Prisma covered her mouth and laughed. It reminded her of her early days working for the Gutter Bitches. She enjoyed that time of her life; it was fun and rebellious until she became jaded and tired of being taken advantage of. "I can't believe this is happening right now. He's so . . . good."

The Doc sipped his water, impressed, but he thought Prisma was ten times better and he didn't want her to start drinking. She would become a handful. "Prisma, you should get up on stage and sing."

Prisma shrank in her seat. She hadn't sung in front of a crowd in years. "No. I mean I . . . I can't. What if I mess up?"

"You have a great voice. There's nothing to be ashamed of. Everyone would love it."

"What do you think, Mr. Watts?" Prisma asked.

"If the Doc is right, which I believe he is, then you should sing. I would love to hear your voice. I'm sure it's magnificent."

Prisma blushed. "Okay. I'll do it."

Bug-eyes finished singing and everybody cheered so loudly the whole saloon shook from the clapping and cheers.

The man covered in white scarves stepped out from the shadows and shoved the bug-eyed man off the stage.

The crowd cheered twice as loud as before.

Bug-eyes lifted himself from the sticky ground and limped back to his seat.

"Who's next? Will it be you? Or you?" He pointed a thick grubby finger at a random guy who wore a ratty cowboy hat. "Well how about you?"

His eyes scanned the crowd and stopped. His finger quickly followed and just so happened to point in Prisma's direction.

Prisma looked around, feigning ignorance.

"You have to get up there," Doc said. "Everyone wants to hear you."

As if on cue, the crowd yelled and cheered for her to get on stage. A drunken man wearing a black beanie shouted, "Get the Gutter Bitch up there!"

More people joined in, raising their drinks and slamming their fists down on wooden tables. "Gu-tter Bitch. Get on stage and show us your tits."

Prisma scanned the crowd for familiar faces and the shadowed sneers evoked memories of pudgy fingers and hot, rank breath on her body. She slowly walked up to the stage, feeling a multitude of eyes fucking her slim curves, and she clasped her sweaty fingers around the microphone.

"I have a feeling this is going to be good," the scarved man said.

Prisma grabbed a white Fender guitar off the ground and wrapped it around her chest diagonally. She strummed a few chords and cleared her throat. "I call this number 'Crystals'." She closed her eyes and sang.

Her vocals were soft and airy. A soft cloud that crept up on you like a dreamy haze.

"In a plastic world, I see crystal clear,
Past the darkness, past the veneer.
I watch you shine like crystals my dear."

She opened her eyes and smiled at Mr. Watts as she continued to sing. He felt something inside him crack and it felt like a warm relief.

Then a shot rang out and the singing stopped.

11.

Erratic gunfire blasted out the shadows, spraying the stage. Shells rained down on the floor.

People swarmed out the bar with hands covering unprotected heads. A rugged barrel-chested man tripped over an overturned stool and fell. A couple people slipped on the wet floor and were trampled to death beneath heavy soles running toward the door.

The scarved man writhed to the right of the stage, bleeding profusely from a gut wound. He gripped a small 9mm pistol in his shaking hand. His scarf slipped from his mouth and revealed myriad scars. In his other hand he held a concave shell to his ear.

"I can hear the ocean . . . it's beautiful."

Prisma delicately stepped over him and hopped off the stage. Mr. Watts snatched her hand and they both ran, careful not to step on anyone or slip on the floor, which was drenched in blood and alcohol. Mr. Watts's light pulsed neon green as adrenaline surged through his veins.

Another shot whizzed past them, embedding itself in Elvis Presley's third eye and the vintage portrait fell to the ground. Glass shattered.

The Doc stood by the door, gesturing for them to hurry their asses up.

Mr. Watts and Prisma raced outside with Doc leading the way and continued running until they were beyond the town's limits. Even from the edge of town, the sound of gunshots popping off like fireworks could be heard.

"What the hell is going on?" Prisma asked.

"I'm unsure. Sounds like a massacre though."

"Someone must be upset," Mr. Watts said.

"Did you think it was my singing?" Prisma asked.

The Doc waved her off. "Let's slow down here. If the shots were directed at us we wouldn't be standing here. You were barely able to sing a couple bars."

Prisma nodded. "Are we going to see your gypsy friend? Because frankly, your pit stops kind of suck and I'm not too fond of getting shot at."

The Doc laughed. "Don't worry. We're heading straight to her place. It's still a little ways off, but I believe we'll make it there in one piece."

Mr. Watts's light pulsed a scarlet red. He was angry they had to leave and frustrated the show was cut short and he wasn't able to absorb the enormity of Prisma's voice. It was a shame he wasn't able to put his hands on the mystery shooter. He would've . . .

Prisma felt a strange tension emanating from the silent Mr. Watts. She went to touch his head and cried out in pain, burning her hand. She shoved her red fingers into the snow and sighed with relief.

"What the hell?" Prisma said, inspecting her fingers.

"I-I'm not sure what happened," Mr. Watts said. "My most sincere apologies. I let my anger get the best of me. I hope I didn't hurt you."

Prisma was slightly turned on by the aggressive side of Mr. Watts. She'd always been attracted to bad boys, even though he was a little different than her usual fare. "I'm fine. Don't worry about it. I'll make sure not to touch you next time you turn red."

"I turned red? I didn't even notice it." Mr. Watts felt his head, which was his normal yellow. "Have I returned to my normal color?"

"Yeah," Prisma said as she came over and caressed his head, putting him at ease.

"Let's get going."

12.

The three of them cautiously approached the old cabin. The house was made out of large, sturdy logs, and the roof was covered in layers of snow.

Rusty bells covered in ice chimed in the wind.

Mr. Watts inadvertently shook and noticed something black twitching in the snow.

"What is that?"

The Doc carefully approached the object and the lines in his forehead deepened considerably.

"It's a dead crow. Bad omen," the Doc said.

"Fuck," Prisma said as she stared at the oversized crow. It had three beady eyes and its wings were slick with ice cold water.

"Normally I wouldn't condone that kind of language," Mr. Watts said, "but this is a rare exception. Prisma is right—Fuck."

Prisma chuckled.

"Mr. Watts, I thought you were a gentleman?" the Doc said. "I know things don't look good, but you should keep your composure at all times—especially, now."

"You're right," Mr. Watts placed his hand over his heart. "My most sincere apologies. I was taken aback."

"Apology accepted," the Doc said.

The crow's wings flapped in the snow as death overtook it and ice began to form inside its veins . . .

The Doc knocked on the door and looked back at Mr. Watts and Prisma.

The door slowly opened. An old, wrinkled hand emerged from the darkness and pulled the door completely open. An ancient-looking woman with hair black as a horse's mane and dark rings underneath her watery eyes inspected the trio on her doorstep.

"Come inside . . . I've been waiting long enough."

They made their way inside the warm interior and were met by the sweet smell of cinnamon and spices from a faraway land.

"Take your shoes off at the door. I was just cooking dinner before you arrived." She picked up a large wooden spoon and licked it suggestively.

Prisma looked away in disgust.

"Your home is lovely, Nadya," Doc said. "It's been a while, to say the least."

"No home or country to call my own. Komodromi blood flows through my veins. Old blood. I'm meant to roam the land like all gypsies do. You're lucky to have found me when you did. I was thinking about going west. This region tires me."

"It seems we're all on the move. How have you been?"

"Well, the world has gotten much colder and a little darker, but besides that I'm doing all right. For some reason clients still seek me out, despite the harsh weather."

"It's no wonder. You're one of the best and we traveled all the way down here to return a favor to my friend Mr. Watts. He saved Prisma from the Gutter Bitches. I owe it to him."

Nadya laughed heartily. "Only two types of people come to see me. The desperate and the foolish. Which one are you?"

Doc swallowed hard as he felt a muddy tension fill the room.

Nadya laughed. It sounded like a frog was caught in her throat. "You don't have to answer that question. I joke. You know I find the strangest things amusing— especially flattery—but I do appreciate compliments. Before we continue, please introduce me to your friends."

The Doc took off his glasses and wiped them with his shirt. "I'm sure you already know who they are. By any rate I guess we'll run through the motions. This here on my left is Prisma and this fine gentleman to my right is Mr. Watts."

Nadya shook Prisma's hand and Mr. Watts's, squeezing a bit too hard for comfort. "It's a pleasure to meet you."

Mr. Watts shook his hand and muttered, "Fuck."

Nadya looked at Mr. Watts as his light turned indigo and he apologized.

Nadya waved him off. "No need to be nervous. Take a seat, make yourselves at home. Dinner's almost ready. We can discuss important matters, like the future and destiny over food and drinks."

Mr. Watts, Prisma, and the Doc did as they were instructed. All of them sat down at the large oak table. Wild, yet elaborate figures were engraved into the table's smooth surface. A variety of wooden spoons hung from the ceiling, swaying ever so slightly.

For some odd reason, the spoons made Mr. Watts uncomfortable.

Nadya grabbed four plates and stacked them with

fat, juicy polar bear steaks—a rare delicacy. She placed one in front of everybody and pulled up a seat at the head of the table.

"Hold on. Need to grab one more thing." Nadya got up and disappeared into the kitchen, slamming and opening cabinet doors.

She came back and carefully set down a jar full of fireflies. "There we go. Now we can eat."

Prisma glanced at the jar and felt bad for the fireflies trapped inside. They emanated a strong neon green light and struck the glass walls, desperately searching for an exit.

Mr. Watts looked down at his plate with great apprehension. He cut into the meat and blue blood oozed out. Must've been cooked rare. He didn't mind, but he worried about making a mess and possibly staining his suit. It was the only one he owned.

"Don't be scared. Dig in before our big discussion. You'll be needing the energy. You have an arduous journey ahead of you."

Prisma looked at Mr. Watts and shrugged. She cut off a small chunk of meat and shoved it in her mouth. Her eyes were expressionless, but after some careful chewing, a slight grin developed.

Mr. Watts took a deep breath and stuffed a piece in his mouth. Explosive flavor, subtle seasoning.

Everyone went to work devouring their hearty meals.

Mr. Watts burped and turned red with embarrassment. "Excuse me."

Nadya rubbed her plump belly and laughed. Copper jewelry hanging off her wrists and ears jangled. "You're excused."

She wiped her mouth and took care of the plates,

placing them in the sink. She grabbed a small wooden spoon before sitting down.

She licked it with her obscenely long tongue, making sure not to miss a single inch, and her eyes rolled into the back of her head—entire body shaking with orgasmic spasms of ecstasy.

Bewildered, Prisma and Mr. Watts looked at each other and then the Doc. However, his eyebrows simply furrowed and his spectacles fogged over.

After an undeterminable amount of time passed, Nadya put the spoon down and took a deep breath.

"Awww, now down to business. I know you didn't travel this far just to have dinner, even though I do cook a mean steak. Now what would you like to know? The future is full of surprises . . . "

The Doc cleared his throat and spread his hands out. "Well, what is to come? Tell us everything."

Nadya chuckled. "Everything? *Everything* revolves around this fellow." She pointed a long finger at Mr. Watts.

Mr. Watts flinched as if Nadya's gnarled index finger would inflict some terrible harm. "Why me?"

"You are special—more special than you would be inclined to believe. However, the future is bleak."

Prisma chimed in. "How bleak is bleak?"

Nadya rapped her longs fingers on the table, each one decked out in exquisite turquoise gold rings. "Very. You see—Mr. Watts—time is running out. Your bright light will not last much longer, unless you find a replacement." Nadya paused dramatically and observed Mr. Watts with her hawk-like eyes.

Mr. Watts cringed, uncomfortable with being the main topic of discussion.

"Mr. Watts ultimately has two options. One: he

can find a replacement lightbulb, or two: seek out his creator. Both of which are formidable tasks to accomplish, and neither odds are in his favor."

"You're saying this whole thing is pointless? We shouldn't even try?" Prisma asked. She was seething with anger.

"Sit your ass down, Prisma. There is still hope. Even in our darkest hour, there is still time for hope. However, this will be dangerous—and—painful."

"What are we supposed to do?" the Doc asked.

"Travel down south and you will find the answers you seek."

"South . . . " The Doc rubbed his pointy chin, pondering the possibility.

"Doc, there is the slim possibility that you might be able to have your old hands return to their former selves, regain that youthful power. And Prisma, your voice can do a lot of good for this world. All of you possess the potential to bring light back into this dark world."

"Is this true?"

"Yes. As a matter of a fact, all your dreams can come true. All you have to do is find the Creator."

Everyone nodded, letting their heads swell with visions of the future.

"Have you heard of craniology my dear?" Nadya asked, turning her attention back to Mr. Watts.

Mr. Watts shook his head. "I'm afraid not."

"Afraid not? You should be." She sipped her wine. "You see, craniology is the scientific study concerning the shape and size of skulls of different human races. I wonder what archaeologists will say when they find yours."

Mr. Watts dropped his glass and quickly cleaned up the spilled contents.

"Well I've tired myself with all this talk of the future and fate. I'm hitting the sack. If you need me, just knock. I'm always available." She winked at the Doc and licked her chapped lips.

"Goodnight Nadya."

"Make yourselves at home and—oh yeah—don't let the Telemarketers bite." This time she winked at Mr. Watts and grabbed a couple of big spoons before departing into her room.

Prisma clenched her fists. "Why did she do that? That was so unnecessary."

"Don't worry about her. Get some sleep. By the sound of it, we have some long days ahead of us."

"All right, but if she says anything else remotely disrespectful I don't know if I'll be able to contain myself."

The Doc made himself at home, snuggling into the contours of a brown loveseat.

Prisma and Mr. Watts eyed the couch.

"I'll sleep on the floor. A lady should never have to rest her head on the ground," said Mr. Watts.

"Mr. Watts, you better lay down on this couch. We're both adults and no one should sleep on the goddamn floor."

" . . . Okay."

Prisma and Mr. Watts lay together on the couch, side by side. Prisma moved closer and placed her arm over his shoulder, bringing him closer, increasing the warmth. Mr. Watts was tense, but eventually loosened up and drifted off to sleep.

A firefly flew woozily inside the glass jar as its cold light flickered and went out.

14.

Mr. Watts woke to a series of screams. Prisma, hands cradling her oval face, stood in the kitchen screaming.

A fully nude Nadya, with rolls of doughy fat and saggy pointed tits, struggled to breathe as the Doc choked her. She dug her nails—more like yellowed claws—into his crooked back, ripping long gashes in his shirt and breaking the skin. He howled in pain, but kept a firm grip on her scrawny neck.

Beads of sweat dripped down his forehead and settled on the tip of his nose. Nadya gasped desperately for air, banging her flabby arms and legs on the wooden floor.

The Doc squeezed harder, his knuckles turning white as snow until there was an audible snap.

Nadya's grey eyes rolled into the back of her head and she slumped over.

The Doc heavily sighed and wiped the sweat from his forehead. "Good Riddance."

Mr. Watts cautiously approached the Doc. "Are you okay Doc?"

"Believe so. Just need to catch my breath."

"What the hell . . . just happened?" Prisma asked.

The Doc stood up, looking down at his hands.

"The bitch tried to rape me. I think she grew tired of her spoon fetish."

Prisma covered her mouth, trying to contain her laughter.

The Doc casually made his way into the kitchen and opened a drawer. "What? I'm a good looking man for my age. Who wouldn't want to rape me?"

Doubt stirred in Prisma's eyes. She placed her hands on her hips and burst into gut-wrenching laughter.

The Doc shrugged and walked over to Nadya's still body. He brought a thick blade down, severing Nadya's head from her neck. Dark red gushed out and blood splattered across the Doc's face.

Prisma stopped laughing.

The Doc stared into Prisma's eyes and flashed a wolfish grin.

15.

Mr. Watts, the Doc, and Prisma made their way through the snow and a cold mist hit them. They stumbled backward, struggling to keep their balance.

Prisma grunted. "I hate the snow."

The Doc nodded. "Don't have to remind me."

Mr. Watts had to get a question out of his head. It had been bothering him all day. "Excuse me Doc, would you be kind enough to explain why we need to bring that head with us?"

The Doc glanced down at the hay sack he was lugging over his shoulder like a trendy fashion accessory. The bottom was soaked in blood and dripped fat red drops into the snow.

"This may seem unsavory, but it's crucial to our success. Decapitated heads used to serve as a legal tool used by noblemen. Always good to keep things handy, and this will come in handy much sooner than you think."

Mr. Watts nodded, even though he had no idea how a decapitated head would ever come in handy and questioned the nobility of these said men.

Scathing gusts of wind blew snow into Mr. Watts's already raw face. Prisma cringed every time the wind touched her exposed skin and the Doc gritted his teeth as he grew numb.

"This wind is fucking terrible. I wish it would stop." Wetness welled up in Prisma's tear ducts.

The Doc noticed Prisma's pain and felt that old heart of his ache with something akin to compassion.

"Okay. We'll find somewhere to stay for the night. I think we could benefit from some rest."

They continued on for another mile until they came across an old cave. It was a bit warmer than the outside world and the humidity was a welcome change.

Sharp stalactites hung from the ceiling, dripping water. The sound of light snores drifted out of the darkness.

The Doc adjusted his spectacles and motioned for everyone to stop. Mr. Watts and Prisma stood frozen, staring into the gloom.

Mr. Watts breathed heavily. He gripped his chest, expecting his rapidly beating heart to explode any second now.

The snores stopped for a brief moment, but thankfully resumed the next. They sounded like harp strings being plucked softly by delicate hands.

Mr. Watts let out a heavy sigh of relief. The snores were beautiful and calmed him. His heart beat slowed down and returned to normal.

The Doc shot Mr. Watts and Prisma a serious look and whispered, "We should leave *carefully*. Not sure what we're dealing with. Soft feet now." He took a few measured steps—stopped—and turned around. "I said *soft* feet."

The Doc led the way toward the exit. Prisma followed closely behind, imagining herself walking on clouds rather than uneven ground. She looked back to see if Mr. Watts was still behind her.

Mr. Watts trailed closely. Close enough to smell her. Tip-toeing, he kept looking behind him, gazing into the darkness. He couldn't hear the snores and longed for their musicality.

He worried and began hyperventilating.

Prisma looked at him and mouthed the words 'hurry up.'

Mr. Watts nodded and took a shaky step forward. His face tingled and he felt weak. He tripped over a branch, falling face-first into snow. Prisma and the Doc reached out to stop him, but were too late.

There was an agonizing silence followed by a rustling in the darkness. Someone yawned—a number of someones.

Multiple voices rang out from the darkness. Harmonized frequencies. "Who dare wake us from our slumber?"

Four angels with hourglass figures and flawless faces flew out from the darkness—soaring overhead. They were naked for the most part and their golden skin shimmered in Mr. Watts's light. Privates were covered in snow bras and panties.

The Doc shielded his eyes from their blinding light and ducked down, covering his head.

One angel flew at Mr. Watts, screaming bloody murder. Her eyes were bloodshot, but her screams were lovely and comforting.

Mr. Watts ducked down and threw his hands in front of his curved face, preparing for the painful collision that was sure to happen.

The snow angel melted upon impact, sluicing into a golden liquid, running down Mr. Watts's face. He shook her wet remains off.

"Disgusting," he said.

Two angels dueled with Doc, trying to back him into a corner. Despite this disadvantage, he swung his hay sack at the angels' glorious heads like a rabid baseball player focused on hitting the home run of a lifetime. After a few misses, he finally made contact with one angel's head—a swift swing that would've put Babe Ruth to shame—and she went flying into a wall, bruising her immaculate face and losing a few teeth in the process.

Prisma screamed at the top of her lungs; she charged the injured angel and kicked her squarely in the jaw. The angel cried out in pain—light growing dim—and slumped over. Mr. Watts rushed over to help, but by the time he reached her, the angel's face was stomped into a bloody pulp.

Prisma grinned. "I think I have this under control. Thanks though."

Mr. Watts shrugged uncomfortably. "I see."

The Doc bent over a teary-eyed angel, biting his lip with concentration. He hacked away at the angel's neck, having a rough time cutting through the wiry tendons. Golden light poured out from the wound rather than blood.

"Whatever happened to the last angel?" Mr. Watts asked, staring upward into the darkness.

"Good question. Did she fly away or something?" Prisma asked, hands on her hips.

"Oh, the last angel? I lit that bitch on fire." The Doc grinned and a shadow crossed his old face.

An angel flew out from the depths of the cave, leaving a fiery trail in her wake. She clawed at the air, thinking it could keep her from falling. Eventually gravity grabbed her in its unmerciful clutches and pulled her down with a *crunch*.

The Doc licked his bloody lips and brought his blade down even harder, picking up the speed and fervor of hacks.

Mr. Watts walked to the angel's charred body. He waved the smoke from his face and upturned his nose once the smell of decay hit entered his nostrils.

The Doc picked up the angel's decapitated head by its long golden locks and slipped it inside his hay sack. It seemed to double in size. He tossed it over his shoulder and with a grunt managed to shoulder the weight.

Prisma looked at the angels' dead bodies and back at Mr. Watts and the Doc. "Are we still staying here for the night?"

The Doc took the hay sack off his shoulder with relief. "Yes, we most certainly are staying the night. I think we earned it."

Prisma beamed. "Good."

Everyone split up in search of kindling and wood. In no time a small fire was made, throwing shadows on the cavernous walls.

The Doc snuggled up into a ball next to the fire and covered himself with a small fleece blanket he brought with him. He snored lightly and muttered incoherent phrases in his sleep.

Mr. Watts moved over to where Prisma was sitting. She quickly wiped a tear from her cheek, sniffled, and her pale face turned red.

"Are you okay Prisma?"

Prisma wiped her nose, smiled, and hugged Mr. Watts. Her sweet aroma was close to overwhelming.

"It's just hard waking up every day not seeing the sun. I have memories, glimpses into the past, but sometimes they feel like a burden rather than a gift. I used to have these vivid dreams . . . the sun beaming in the sky and all of sudden it began to deteriorate like a strip of film burning up . . . crackling . . . black bubbles forming on the surface. It was horrifying."

"What happened next?" Mr. Watts asked.

"Everything went black."

The fire crackled nearby.

"I'm just . . . sick and tired of seeing darkness . . . but you're here now. This little light of mine." She hummed a distant yet familiar tune.

She rubbed Mr. Watts's head and stared into the depths of his eyes.

He felt wonderful, swimming in the purple sea that was Prisma's eyes. At his most calm state of mind, his worries and troubles fell away like a second skin and his light turned a lemon yellow.

Prisma grabbed Mr. Watts's tie in her fist and pulled him closer. She began to loosen the knot and unbutton his shirt.

Mr. Watts grew nervous and he started to back away. "It's getting really warm in here."

"It's okay Mr. Watts. Let me do all the work."

Mr. Watts stammered. "U-um . . . okay . . . I guess."

Prisma pushed him down on her thin sleeping bag and pulled his pants off and carefully placed his dress shoes to the side. Then she eased her fingers into the elastic of his pin-striped boxers and pulled them down, revealing his throbbing cock.

She went down on his cock, working the shaft and running her tongue around the head. Mr. Watts moaned.

Prisma climbed on top of him and slid his cock into her wet vagina. She rode him, doing most of the work and smoothly rolled into missionary. Mr. Watts thrusted into her wet pussy, forgetting about his past, forgetting the frigid cold outside, forgetting the depression that grew overwhelming at times, the fact that he was freak with a lightbulb for a head, and enjoyed the all-consuming pleasure of the moment, the ecstasy of now. His tungsten filament thrummed with a powerful current and he climaxed in a blinding light.

Prisma curled up with Mr. Watts, basking in his warmth.

16.

A naked lightbulb—suspended from the ceiling—swayed slowly side to side.

Mr. Watts rolled around, trying to break outside the confines of his crib. He reached for the light, baby hands outstretched . . . straining.

The light continued to sway, but now began to spin in slow, hypnotic circles.

Mesmerized and even more desperate to grab the beaming light and hold it in his small hands, Mr. Watts stood up and strained twice as hard, doubling his efforts.

He fell backwards and his diaper cushioned his fall.

Sad and depressed, Mr. Watts cried himself to sleep.

17.

Mr. Watts woke up, feeling displaced, and Prisma lay in his arms, nuzzling him like a cat.

Doc sauntered over, wiping the sleep from his wrinkled eyes. "Okay lovebirds, time to hit the road. We should be able to make it to the river today."

"What river?" Mr. Watts asked.

"The river Styx," the Doc replied.

Mr. Watts nodded even though he had no conception of what or where this river was located.

Prisma and the Doc gathered their things and then all three of them made their way outside into the frigid darkness.

They walked and walked and walked some more, and just when they thought they were done walking, they had to walk some more.

Finally, they stopped to rest their weary legs.

Prisma bit into a chocolate bar and cocked her head sideways. "Do you hear that?"

"What?" Mr. Watts asked.

"Someone's playing music."

The Doc wiped the fog from his spectacles. "Sounds familiar."

"It's beautiful," Mr. Watts proclaimed.

Mr. Watts turned his eyes towards the darkness,

waiting for the mystery musician to make their appearance known.

The musician rolled out of the darkness in an old-fashioned brown blazer and matching brown pants. He seemed to glide from one point to the next—never once touching the ground—growing transparent one moment and returning to his former self the next.

"Oh my God, he has two fucking heads," Prisma said.

One head was covered in coarse uncombed brown hair, and long frizzy brown hair draped down the other. The two-headed musician held a pristine violin in his fat, knobby hands and played a frenzied composition of beautiful—yet haunting—notes which floated on thin air.

"It can't be," the Doc said in awe.

"What?" Mr. Watts said in anticipation.

"It's Mozathoven, the ghost of Mozart and Beethoven. Legend has it that they haunted a rural region of the south, playing their lost concerto in the arctic cold. But I didn't think the legend could possibly be true. It's been years since I've heard a single piece of classical music. This is absolutely wonderful."

A solitary tear slid down the Doc's face, turned into ice and disappeared into the ground.

Mr. Watts patted the Doc on the back while he watched the performance unfold.

As Mozathoven skipped around and finished the musical piece, one head (belonging to Mozart) began to shake and snot flowed out of his nostrils. Mozathoven dropped down on all fours, dropping the instrument in the snow. With an arched back, he cried out in agonizing pain as their noses elongated into wet snouts and upper body muscles cracked as they grew bigger and stronger. Thick tufts of hair sprouted from their enlarged pores and Mozathoven howled as the tattered brown blazer slipped off like a shell.

Mozathoven stood up in all of his glory and slowly became indistinguishable as he faded away into nothingness. The only thing that remained were the musty pheromones padding the air.

The Doc whispered, "Wolfgang."

Prisma took a step back and said, "Wow."

The Doc gathered himself and cleared his ragged throat. "Wow is right, but we need to get this show back on the road. Who knows how close that Telemarketer could be?"

As they continued on their journey, the Doc looked back one last time, hoping to catch another glimpse of his favorite composers, but all he saw was a blanket of darkness.

18.

Mr. Watts wasn't sure how close they were to the river. The only thing he knew for certain was the aching pain raging inside the soles of his feet. He bit his lip and fought through it and noticed the same weariness burrowing its way into Prisma and the Doc. He wondered how much farther they could travel before they dropped from exhaustion or pneumonia.

The sound of running water trickled in the distance and Prisma's bowed head lifted.

"Is that the river?" Mr. Watts asked, hoping he would get a yes.

"It should be," the Doc said. "There's a few others, but even if our path was incorrect this should be the one."

"I really hope so. My legs are killing me," Prisma said, stretching her body.

After about another mile or so, the raging river made itself known. Water flowed incredibly fast down the banks, splashing cold drops onto the frozen bank. Sharp, jagged rocks lined the shore well into the blurry horizon.

"Don't get too close," the Doc advised. "Might slip. Wait a moment."

"For what?" Mr. Watts asked.

"You'll see." The Doc flashed a grin.

A cold draft blew by, ruffling the trio. Mr. Watts shivered uncontrollably.

A pinpoint of light shone in the distance, growing brighter and doubling in intensity. It revealed a weathered wooden boat—constructed from sequoia trees—coasting toward the shore. A sinewy old man with an incredibly long beard—housing caterpillars and dead leaves—captained the vessel. He took his gnarled staff and stabbed it into the snowy bank and the boat came to a standstill. On top of the staff sat a small gas light with a fat candle burning inside.

"Do you wish to cross?" the old man croaked.

Mr. Watts looked into the old man's feverish eyes and shook with fear. Fear of what lay beyond the river, and a creeping fear that he was one step closer to the Creator threatened to disturb his existential make-up.

"Yes," the Doc replied without hesitation.

The Doc handed over the hay sack containing the gypsy's head as well as the angel's. And even after all this time, the bottom of the sack still dripped copious amounts of blood.

The old man grabbed the hay sack, dropped it at his feet, and fished Nadya's head out. He appraised it carefully, spinning it with his hands. Once satisfied, he grunted and placed the head back in the hay sack and set it down beside him.

Then he pulled the angel's head out by its golden locks and his eyes widened as he stroked her cheeks with a strange appreciation. He kissed her cold lips and reluctantly placed it back inside.

"Your token of passage is more than acceptable. Come aboard."

The Doc stepped on the small boat followed by Prisma and Mr. Watts. The boat rocked, and settled down after everyone took a seat.

The old man wrapped his long, scarred fingers around his staff and solemnly stared into the distance. The boat began to move with the tide. The wind helped move it along and they picked up speed.

Mr. Watts held on to the side of the boat for dear life, hoping the ride would be relatively short. He couldn't remember the last time he'd been out to sea, let alone on a boat. His head hurt and his stomach bubbled with the promise of nausea.

Darkness surrounded them and anguished moans began to fill the air.

The old man fished Nadya's head out of the hay sack, scrutinized its wizened face, and tossed it into the river.

"Goodbye my friend. May the afterlife treat you well."

What purpose did that serve? Mr. Watts thought.

Mr. Watts stared at the calm water and jumped back when the quiet was disturbed by splashing and the sound of loud, reckless chewing beneath the surface. Old rotten teeth chewed through decayed skin and smacked on gristle and fat, ripping through bone to reach soft, sweet marrow.

Mr. Watts looked to Prisma for some sort of reassurance, but all he found were sorrowful eyes staring back at him—reflecting his inner thoughts.

"That should hold em' off a while," said the old man, wiping his dirty hands on his robe.

A geyser of blood shot up from the dark water, barely missing the boat's bow, and disappeared into the sky.

Mr. Watts slumped down next to Prisma and she buried her face in his arms, clutching him close.

The Doc stared into the distance as if he was scrying future events—already knowing what was going to happen from day one.

Leftover moans still rose from the darkness like fragmented dreams, but faded away with time.

Soon enough the boat reached the end of the river.

"Here we are."

The Doc thanked the old man and stepped off the boat. Prisma and Mr. Watts followed suit.

The old man nodded, petting the hay sack appreciatively, and his boat began to float away and the darkness swallowed him whole.

19.

The river Styx was still and eerily quiet. Thick branches coursed down its surface and a few dead souls leaped in the air and dove back down into the water.

The water stirred and out of the depths a Telemarketer rose, buzzing with static and raw anger. He crawled onto the shore on all fours—thousands of dead souls hanging off him.

The Telemarketer brushed the dead souls off, frowned at the inconvenience, and stomped them into the snow where they twitched out of existence. He cherished their death rattle. It more than made up for the black fluid trickling from his wounds, staining his white cuffs.

The Telemarketer sniffed the air; a smile stretched across his face, and he howled into the darkness.

Black static rang through the night.

20.

How much longer until we reach this place?" Prisma asked.

The Doc thought it over. "Not too much longer. We should actually be able to make it there today."

"Phew," said Prisma as she wiped sweat from her brow. "I cannot wait to get there and rest my legs."

"You think you need to rest your legs? Wait until you reach my age. Stiff joints, bad knees. You name it, I got it."

Prisma laughed. "That'll be a while."

"It'll be here sooner than you think. Life is short. It seems long at times, but it moves with a frightening quickness."

"Thanks for the life lesson, Doc." Prisma rolled her eyes.

The Doc shrugged.

"Do you think we'll actually find a spare lightbulb?" Mr. Watts asked, rubbing his head.

"Honestly, I can't say yes or no, but we'll find something. Be it the Creator or a spare lightbulb."

"I hope you're right."

"I hope so too. If the Creator actually exists, perhaps I can get these blasted hands of mine fixed once and for all."

The Doc looked down at his wrinkled hands as if

84

they were foreign objects, once loved and cherished, but now worn-out relics.

"And maybe I could . . . " Prisma looked down at her feet sullenly.

"You were saying?" Mr. Watts asked.

"Oh, it's nothing. Just a little thought."

"Just spit it out," said the Doc. "No one is going to judge you."

Prisma took a deep breath. "Well, it's silly—I know—but I always wanted to be a singer. My mom used to be a famous singer before she overdosed. She brought back that *soul*. People loved her and still do. I want to carry on her legacy."

"It doesn't sound silly to me," said the Doc.

"It's a sound endeavor. I'm sure your Mom would be proud," said Mr. Watts.

Prisma laughed nervously. "I think she would be, but it just seems impractical. I mean it may have been possible before the Blackout, but now it just seems pointless to even hope for something like that. What am I going to do? Tour around the tundra on foot and hope I don't get killed . . . or worse?"

"Nothing is pointless," Mr. Watts said. "If you have the talent and the determination, which I'm sure you do, then you might as well give it a try. Otherwise, your dreams will fade away and wither."

"Prisma, he's right. People need something, be it a voice or anything. Like you said; a lot of music is missing soul. People could use that—especially nowadays."

Prisma nodded, rolling the possibility around in her head, toying with the idea until it solidified.

Mr. Watts walked in silence, glancing Prisma's way every now and then. He was growing worried that something unfortunate might happen to her.

He briefly considered slipping off into the darkness and letting Prisma and the Doc return to their former lives. *Perhaps they'll have a greater chance of survival without me slowing them down,* he thought. *And maybe Prisma might even have a legitimate chance of making her dream become reality . . .*

. . . But he realized that would make him a coward; no better than a scroungy mutt. And no gentleman of his stature was a coward. Most certainly not Mr. Watts.

Prisma leaned over, sensing Mr. Watts's mood shifting (chalk it up to a woman's intuition) and kissed him on the cheek, leaving a ghostly impression of her lips on his glass head. His light turned a moody turquoise.

"What's the matter?"

"Nothing. Just thinking about life and such."

"Well don't think too hard." She rubbed his head.

"I'll try not to." Mr. Watts forced a grin.

They trudged on through the snow, but after a while the snow became sloshy and wet. It was becoming easier to move through, and they covered much more territory than they could ever imagine.

Sloshy snow eventually gave way to patches of long, dead grass and weeds.

Mr. Watts bent down and picked a small blossoming rose from the ground. "Prisma."

"What?" Prisma asked as she unbuttoned her coat.

Mr. Watts dramatically bowed and handed her the small rose. It looked pathetic in his hand, but he maintained his grin despite this. "A rose for a rose."

Prisma blushed. "Thank you. You always know how to make a girl blush."

"That's strange," the Doc said. "The snow seems to be melting. With no sunlight that must be close to impossible."

"Maybe it means we're close," Prisma sniffed the rose, awakening old memories of her running through fields.

"That's a strong possibility. Perhaps that would explain the rapid rise in temperature."

Three more steps and a large hulking figure jutted out from the darkness. It was hard to make out, but there were small patches of light in the distance which helped outline the building.

As they got closer, they realized it wasn't a building at all. Instead, it was a massive satellite that seemed to have crashed decades ago. It left a deep impression in the earth's crust—a thawing astrobleme. Snow piled up in large, foreboding hills around it. Random debris littered the ground; a 2003 monster truck brandishing a logo that was smeared out of existence, a dented metal sign that advertised "Red Hot Pete's" with a cartoon hotdog figure waving (or at least he seemed to be waving), and charred office furniture leftover from the top two floors of an office building that was smashed to smithereens by the satellite.

"It has to be the satellite," the Doc said. "Must be emitting some type of radiation or it has some powerful back-up generators. Either way, it's directly affecting the environment," the Doc said.

"Your theory sounds solid," Mr. Watts said.

"We'll see once we get inside," Prisma added.

21

Mr. Watts looked up at the behemoth of a satellite and still couldn't quite comprehend how something like this could ever fall from the sky, let alone float in the cold ether of space.

His nervousness began to wrap its cold fingers around his insides and squeeze. Butterflies hatched inside him, desperate to claw out his stomach.

He closed his eyes, relishing the privacy of his own darkness—took a deep breath—and shook off any bits of timidness that remained.

It's now or never, he thought. *Today is going to be the day I'm going to meet my maker or . . . find a spare lightbulb.*

And he wanted to make a good first impression because first impressions are the most important.

"Are you ready?" Prisma asked.

"Yes, I believe so. Do I look professional and somewhat approachable?" Mr. Watts dusted imaginary dust off his suit and refolded his handkerchief four times before placing it back inside his coat pocket.

"Mr. Watts, you look fine. You're a handsome gentleman."

"Thank you. Honestly, I'm not sure what I'd ever do without you. Who knows? I'd probably still be walking around in the darkness if it wasn't for you—or worse. I could be dead."

Prisma gave him a quick peck that warmed his cold insides.

"Let's go inside. It's freezing out here."

"Okay," Mr. Watts said, still woozy from the kiss.

The Doc pulled on a door, digging his heels into the snow for leverage, but the damn thing wouldn't budge. It had to be permanently stuck or the hinges were frozen.

The Doc wiped sweat off his brow. "Come help me out with this, Mr. Watts. This thing is barely moving or it might not be moving at all. I can't tell with my awful eyesight. Appreciate your youth. It'll be gone before you know it."

Mr. Watts got a solid grip on the door, and both him and the Doc strained their backs and arms, pulling with all their combined might till the door groaned open.

Cold wind blew inside, but a warm gust of air blew out.

"Woah. It's warm in there," Prisma said, loosening her coat.

Thick cable wires and plant life draped down in front of the opening like snakes. The Doc pushed the curtain of foliage aside and ducked inside.

Mr. Watts followed the Doc's example and helped Prisma come inside.

The room was jam-packed with supercomputers and loud modems. Each screen displayed various bits of information and cryptic diagrams. Technology was still running in most parts, yet in other sections Mother Nature seemed to hold sway.

The interior held creeping shadows and caliginous

pockets of darkness. The prominent whirring and beeping of technology set Mr. Watts on edge, and the subtle sounds of exotic wildlife emanated from the depths of the satellite did nothing to dissuade his paranoia.

Patches of grass and vegetation forced their way through the ground and up the cracks in the titanium plated floor. Cables hung from the ceiling haphazardly—some still spitting colorful sparks from rubber mouths.

"This isn't right," the Doc said. "These plants have caused so much damage."

"But it's amazing. Don't you think? The resiliency of these plants. The vibrant life." Prisma touched a gigantic flower and smelled its ambrosial aroma.

It snapped at her and she staggered backwards, nearly losing her precarious footing.

"See, what did I tell you?" the Doc said. "No one listens to the Doc. Oh, he's just a silly old man with a fetish for decapitation. No one remembers the fact that he's a man of science—a healer."

"I'm sorry Doc. I'm wrong. Okay? Hope that makes you feel better." Prisma sulked.

"It's okay. I just want both of you to be careful. We've reached the end of the line and things might get crazy from here on out."

"As if things weren't crazy enough," Prisma said.

A rabid growl rolled out of the shadows and bounced off the metal walls like a ping pong ball.

Cables hissed and snapped.

"We better start moving," the Doc said.

Leaves rustled and plants shook.

"NOWWWWW!" the Doc yelled.

Mr. Watts snatched Prisma's trembling hand and

they booked it towards an open orange door. The Doc followed closely behind, trying his best to keep up.

The door might be locked, but it was a gamble they were willing to take, including Mr. Watts, who rarely dabbled in throwing the odds in fate's hands.

Heavy breathing, harsh fetid breath and the scuttling of claws were too close for comfort.

Mr. Watts whipped the door open, pushed Prisma into the darkness, and turned back for the Doc, but he was gone.

22.

Machines hissed and buzzed in the darkness.

Mr. Watts ran as fast as he possibly could, sweat seeping through his cream-colored tuxedo. He wondered if he was going to live another day. First thing he planned to do was find a reputable dry cleaner and get his suit in order.

The Doc was being dragged by two young white tigers with black stripes covering their fur; sky blue hydrangeas blossomed from their eyes. He wondered how they navigated the jungle.

"Stop—you foul beasts."

One tiger stopped, leaving the other one to handle the job of dragging the Doc by himself. It came forward and released a low, throaty growl and bared its yellowed teeth.

"I'm standing my ground."

The tiger jumped forward and Mr. Watts fell backward, trying to fight the beast off his chest. Out of the corners of his eyes, he saw the Doc get pulled into the darkness and an ear-piercing scream rang out from the vegetation.

Mr. Watts gripped the tiger's wet snout and slammed it into the ground. It was temporarily dazed and surprised by the offensive move.

Mr. Watts ripped the flowers from the tiger's eyes and the tiger cried out in pain, snapping at the air. Blood sputtered out its sockets like a runny red crust.

The mewling tiger walked on wobbly legs into the vegetation, blindly groping for his brother through the greenery.

Mr. Watts ran into the thick vegetation, illuminating the darkness. Wild plant life enclosed him on all sides, a leafy green prison.

"Doc! Where are you?" Mr. Watts shouted, ducking under a prickly man-sized leaf.

A moan rolled out from a bush ahead of him.

Mr. Watts pushed the bush aside and found the Doc. He was lying on his side, attempting to slide his intestines back into his stomach. He was failing miserably.

The Doc groaned in pain, holding up his bloody hands, and squinted at Mr. Watts through his cracked spectacles. He saw a figure surrounded by a halo light. He reached his hand out, stretching with his last bit of strength.

"G-God?"

The Doc's eyes closed and blood trickled out of his mouth. His body became still.

Mr. Watts was speechless. He bent down and grabbed the Doc's cold hands inside his own. "I hope you're in a better place, my friend. You will be forever missed."

A tear streamed down Mr. Watts's glass head and quickly turned to steam. He stood up, concerned about Prisma, and ran back to check on her.

23.

Mr. Watts stepped into the dimly-lit room and the shadows fled from his light. Huge and spacious, the room was incredible in its size and scope. Most of it was untouched by plant life and still in remarkably good shape. In spite of this, a few weeds and patches of crab grass sprouted from a crack in the floor.

None of the machines showed any signs of life or any possible resurrection. Some were smashed beyond repair and others were ridden with rust. Orange and red flakes peppered the already dirty ground.

It was strange to be greeted by silence.

"Prisma! Where are you?" Mr. Watts yelled. "Prismaaaaa!" His voice cracked and echoed, bouncing off the metal walls.

"I'm right here." Prisma slipped out of the shadows, discarding it like a silky gown. She clutched a large rusty pipe. "Is everything all right?"

"Where did you get that?"

Prisma looked down at the pipe in her hand like it was nothing more than a toy and laughed. "Oh this—well—it's something I found while I was waiting on you. A girl's gotta have protection."

Mr. Watts's light turned pine green—a little

94

freaked out that Prisma was ready to resort to violence.

"Where's the Doc at?" she asked. "Is he taking his sweet time or something?"

Mr. Watts said nothing and looked away.

"Oh no. It's written all over your face. He didn't . . . he's . . . no . . . he can't be." Prisma collapsed in Mr. Watts's arms, sobbing into his chest.

He stroked her soft hair, not sure what to say. Words couldn't fix the situation no matter how well-read of a gentleman he was. He stood there, rubbing the middle of her back, and let her cry.

She looked up and wiped her eyes. "What are we going to do?"

"We can continue looking for the Creator. I assume that's what the Doc would have wanted."

Prisma sniffled. "I think you're right. But where do we go from here?"

"We have to keep looking and searching. There's life here. Maybe somebody is still around. Someone who could tell us something of value."

"That's sort of a stretch isn't it?"

"Well this is all guesswork on my part. I think it's still worth striving for. In the end, we can at least say we tried."

"I guess so . . . " She blinked the tears away, but her melancholy coated her aura in a dark haze.

Mr. Watts held her hand and his light turned sky blue. He could feel her warm steady pulse match his own. It gave him comfort and security and—above all else—it provided him with the motivation to keep going.

They walked farther into the room, searching the shadows for any other life, and carefully avoided any plants in case they housed white tigers or something equally dangerous.

The halls went on for what seemed like forever.

"Where the hell are we going?" Prisma asked.

"What do you mean?" Mr. Watts asked.

Prisma pulled her hand away and brushed her hair away from her ear. "This place . . . it's absurd. We're wasting our time. You can keep looking for this imaginary Creator, but I'm leaving."

There was a slight chuckle and a hand shot out from the darkness and closed itself around Prisma's mouth. Another hand popped out, brandishing a plasma gun aimed directly at Prisma's head.

"I'm sorry to inform you, but you're not going anywhere."

24.

"**Let her go** at once," Mr. Watts said.

The mysterious man stepped out from the shadows, revealing a gold-toothed grin, an unkempt black Mohawk, and a soiled lab coat which housed an overweight figure.

Prisma struggled in the man's grip, but she stopped once he shoved the plasma gun against her temple.

He laughed. "You're not the man with the gun in your hands, are you?"

Mr. Watts said nothing and his light turned a Venetian red.

"And you're not the man holding this girl's life in his hands. Are you?"

No response.

"That would be a no." The man removed the gun from Prisma's temple, ran it through her hair, and traced its cold mouth down her chest all the way to her navel.

"Now that we know who's calling the shots, let me tell you how things are going to be. First of all, you two aren't supposed to be here. You were supposed to be killed off days ago."

Mr. Watts finally said something. "But how?"

"Oh, now Mr. Lightbulb Head wants to speak up. How nice of you to grace us with your voice. Remember the karaoke bar? I hired a man with a penchant for wearing a white scarf to kill you, but he failed miserably. The imbecile ended up dead at his own expense."

The man paused as if all this talking was exasperating. "Now I have to kill you two myself. I hate getting my hands dirty. Being a scientist and all, I hate killing off my guinea pigs, but sadly I must terminate this one."

Prisma moaned.

Mr. Watts sprang forward, ready to attack.

The man aimed his gun directly at Mr. Watts. It glowed a pulsating green, and the man played with the trigger, ready to pull it any second.

"That wouldn't be very wise. Now, I suggest you step back and do whatever I say."

Mr. Watts nodded.

"Both of you are going to walk in front of me while I keep this nice gun aimed at your heads. You keep walking until I say stop. Understand?"

Mr. Watts nodded.

"How about you?" The man tapped Prisma's head with his gun and she cringed.

She moaned and nodded quickly.

"I'll take that as a yes."

The scientist led them down a hallway they had never seen before. It was small, dark, and claustrophobic. A rat with three tails scurried by and Prisma shrieked, clawing imaginary beasts off her body.

"Bitch! Turn back around and keep walking. A rat is the least of your trouble." The scientist's brown eyes

98

gleamed in the presence of Mr. Watts's sangria red light.

Prisma did as instructed and slowly turned around, scanning the ground for any rats or other critters creeping through the passageway.

They walked for a bit, to the point where neither Mr. Watts nor Prisma remembered the finer points of their journey. Who knows how big this satellite truly is?

"Stop," the man yelled. He walked to a door and keyed in a code. The door *whooshed* open.

"Go inside," he said.

Prisma walked in first, feeling the scientist's greedy eyes molest her back and curves. Growing more pissed by the second, she balled her hands into fists and dug her nails into her palms.

Fucker.

Mr. Watts looked up at the domed ceiling comprised of webbed yellow windows. It loosely resembled a horsefly's eyeball. He glanced down and took in the room. It was similar to the rest of the satellite, in which plant life and technology mingled in a destructive dance, but there was something hanging in the middle of the room, but no matter how hard he strained his eyes, he failed to make out whatever it was.

"Go ahead. Take it in. This will be your coffin, after all."

Prisma grabbed Mr. Watts's cold hand and squeezed.

"It'll be okay," whispered Mr. Watts.

Prisma smiled weakly, and a tear slid down her cheek.

"Enough of the lovey-dovey bullshit. I need both of you to see something. I think you deserve to know."

The scientist walked up to a dark figure and gestured with his gun for them to come over. It glinted as Mr. Watts came closer.

Mr. Watts approached the figure—one step at time—and gasped in horror when a cold realization set it in.

It was the Creator. *His father*. The man they risked life and limb to find—he was dead. Thick serpentine cables and exotic vines wrapped around his neck in a deadly embrace.

"Is that who I think it is?" Mr. Watts asked, surprised to even hear himself utter words in the face of death.

"Yes. It's Noah Steinberg. Your creator, your father—whatever you want to call him."

Mr. Watts held his throbbing head in hands, his mind flush with excavated memories spilling out.

"Is it okay if we go play outside?"

"Ask your big brother if he can watch you. Daddy's working right now."

"Watts, let's go outside," she said in a squeaky voice.

"Spectra, that's no way to talk to your brother. Mind your manners and ask nicely."

"Watts, can you please come outside and watch me play?" She asked, batting her non-existent eyelashes. "Pretty pretty *please* with ice cream on top and lots of cherries."

Busy shining his black dress shoes, Mr. Watts barely registered his sister's question. He looked back down at the shoe in hand and thought it wasn't nearly shiny enough for his liking. He sighed and grabbed his shoe shine kit. "Let's go."

Wearing a straw hat, Mr. Watts sat down in a plastic chair, inspected his reflection in one of his dress shoes and nodded with satisfaction.

"Watty! Watty! Watch me climb this tree," Spectra said as she started climbing up the tree's massive trunk.

"Be careful Spectra," Mr. Watts said. He got back to work on his other shoe, spitting on it before adding a dab of black shoe polish. He rubbed furiously until he began to see the muddiness smooth out.

He looked up and noticed Spectra's little lightbulb head disappearing into the thick branches, and the tree swayed ever so slightly. A group of startled bluebirds flew away from the leafy crown, criss-crossing in geometric patterns.

Spectra, who was covered in small scratches, looked up into the darkness, determined to reach the top of the tree, her own Mount Everest. The neighborhood kids always egged her on, telling her she couldn't do it simply because she was a girl.

I'll show them, she thought as she climbed higher with sweaty hands, gripping a branch to pull her weight up. The branch cracked and she swallowed hard, hoping it wouldn't snap before she could grab something else more solid.

Snap.

Spectra fell through the branches. Bones inside her soft body broke and her glass head fractured and exploded into a fiery rain of glass.

Mr. Watts cast aside his shoes and ran barefoot through the grass. He picked up Spectra's broken body and accidentally stepped in the glass. The pain barely registered as his breath hitched in his chest and he sobbed; he dropped down to his knees and held her close. He never realized how *light* she was, how empty she felt.

His father rushed outside and broke into tears the moment he saw Mr. Watts holding Spectra in his trembling arms.

"I-I thought I told you to watch her," his father snapped. "I can't even compute this."

"I tried."

"You tried? Your sister's dead and that's all you have to say for yourself—*I tried*."

"I apologize . . . I should have paid more attention. Been more aware. I thought . . . I thought . . . "

His father brought his arm around Mr. Watts's quaking shoulders. "Look, it'll be okay. We'll get through this. We're family."

Mr. Watts's face filled his hands and his light grew dim as the crippling realization set in. He was responsible for his sister's death—one step away from murder.

It was his carelessness and obsession with being the perfect gentleman that made this happen. *If only I had listened*, he thought. *Maybe she would still be alive . . .*

He dramatically ripped his silver cuff links out and tossed them to the ground. Then he undid his tie haphazardly and clawed at his jacket, tearing a large gash into his sleeve. White tufts of cotton spilled out. Prisma wrapped her arms around his body, stopping him from doing any further damage. He collapsed into her chest and they melted into the floor.

"I had a sister . . . a father . . . an entire family . . . gone," he whispered, glancing at his father's suspended body, staring into the darkness of his eyes, becoming lost in the void.

Mr. Watts turned back to the scientist. "You did this?"

"No, I promise you I didn't. Shortly after the Great Blackout, my colleagues forced their way inside and there was a . . . brief scuffle. Noah didn't come out on the winning side."

"That doesn't make you innocent, does it now?" Mr. Watts's light turned a livid yellow. "You're just as guilty as the rest of them."

The scientist grew noticeably nervous, taking a step backward. "Look, I'll tell you the truth. Noah was good man and a great scientist—world renowned. After the Blackout he disappeared, falling off the radar. He came here to find a way to bring light back to the world. You were one of his early experiments and as far as we know—his only success."

"Why was he killed? He sounds like great man. I have to know." Mr. Watts's light darkened to seismic orange.

"I'm part of a group of rogue scientists. We wanted the recognition—the fame—of bringing light back to the world. We decided to knock him out of the history books. Just look at Nikola Tesla. People barely know who he is, but he did so much. We wanted to be modern day Edisons. Thought we would be treated like Gods in the new world. At least, that's what we pictured, but things . . . didn't pan out the way we expected."

Prisma backed away from Mr. Watts, her tear-stained face now doused in a flickering red light.

Unfiltered rage filled Mr. Watts's frame and the landscape turned a flush, woozy red.

The scientist wiped the sweat off his face and thought his bladder might give. A tremor ran down his arm as he raised his gun and aimed it at Mr. Watts.

"I didn't want things to end like this—I swear—but . . . "

Someone banged on the door.

"What the hell?" the scientist's brow creased with worry lines and perspiration.

Prisma's head shot up with fear and looked to Mr. Watts for some type of reassurance.

Mr. Watts was too angry, blinded by his own rage to hear the knocking or to notice Prisma.

The banging grew louder with each successive knock.

The scientist waved his gun, aiming it at the door and back at Mr. Watts. He was confused and sweating profusely, wishing he was elsewhere.

Prisma had no idea what to do, so she simply stared at the vibrating door, hoping it would hold strong and whoever was behind it would go away.

These wishful thoughts turned into fear as the rusty hinges popped out one by one, rolling across the floor like gun shells.

The door flew inward, slamming into the scientist's chest. He fell backwards and his gun slipped out his hand, skidding into a corner.

A dust cloud hid the intruder's face. A moment passed and the dust cleared away. The Telemarketer let out an electric hiss.

The hairs on Prisma's neck stood at full attention, and Mr. Watts took note of the Telemarketer's harrowing presence.

The Telemarketer whipped its skinny head backwards, howled, and static filled the room.

Prisma covered her ears, grimacing in pain.

"Prisma, hide!" Mr. Watts shouted, gesturing to the shadows.

She shot him a worried look, but did as she was instructed and scurried into the shadows.

The scientist rolled over and slowly got to his feet. He rubbed his head and his hand came away covered in blood.

"Jesus Christ," he mumbled. He picked his gun up off the ground.

The Telemarketer licked his moist black lips and tightened his grip on his battered briefcase.

The scientist had never dealt with a Telemarketer in his life, except for the normal ones who called you back in the day. Of course he heard of them—everyone did. He thought they were a myth, a story mothers told to their children at night, the conjurings of a rattled mind, but once he realized they existed in three dimensions, he gripped his gun tight.

He aimed it at the Telemarketer and pulled the trigger again and again.

The first few shots missed their mark, embedding themselves in computer monitors and modems. Sparks and flames spat out of the damaged technology.

Thankfully, the next few shots met their mark, tearing through the Telemarketer's chest, leaving big, black gaping wounds. Black fluid sputtered out, splattering the floor.

The Telemarketer staggered back a few steps, clutching his stomach.

Click. Click. Click.

105

The scientist fingered the trigger, desperately wishing it was jammed. That was better than the grim realization that it was empty.

Should've brought an extra charge, but it's too late for that now, isn't it?

The Telemarketer must have read his thoughts because he grinned and bum-rushed the scientist—dipping his head low—arms spread wide. He tackled him, taking him down, and something popped in the scientist's back. It sounded painful.

Mr. Watts watched the Telemarketer pin the scientist down and felt absolutely nothing when he began to scream.

The Telemarketer forced a contract down the scientist's throat, muffling his scream.

"You are now the sole property of me and me alone. You belong to me—body and soul. If you wish to dispute this claim, read the contract you just ate." The Telemarketer's voice sounded like a chaotic mass of black and white static combined with the buzzing of frenzied locusts.

Mr. Watts genuinely feared for his life. There was something not right about the Telemarketer. Its very existence confused and angered him.

It's unnatural, he thought. Maybe the Doc was right. Maybe the Telemarketers really were spawned from darkness and misery and depression.

It made sense.

Mr. Watts looked into the Telemarketer's obsidian black eyes and saw civilizations fall to ruin, soft black stars die, and pale crocodiles snapping their crooked teeth.

Mr. Watts ran in the opposite direction. It was the only sensible thing to do.

Strong arms wrapped around Mr. Watts's stomach and slammed him down on the wet, pulpy ground. He cracked his head on the tile and the air rushed out of his lungs. A small crack formed in his glass head and developed into a fissure, yet his lightbulb held strong.

The Telemarketer pinned Mr. Watts down with his incredibly strong knees, pushing his weight forward.

Mr. Watts cringed in pain, attempting to push the Telemarketer off, but he weighed too much. The world began to swim in and out of focus, blurring at the edges.

Don't give in to the tide, Mr. Watts told himself, fighting desperately to stay conscious. He had to do it for Prisma's sake, do it for the Doc, and avenge his lost father—the Creator.

The Telemarketer calmly unclamped his leather briefcase and pulled out a brochure with lines of gibberish neatly typed out.

"Sign up for this two-hundred year loan. Zero percent interest. No loan sharks. Money in your pocket NOWWWW!!!" The Telemarketer buzzed, waiting for an answer.

Mr. Watts grew angry, remembering the death, the cold and the darkness. His father's stricken face rose in his mind like a ghostly visage and he grew angry. Angry that people would murder a good man, an innocent man. He harnessed this anger until his head surged with a searing rage.

The room turned a vivid, pulsating red.

The Telemarketer hissed and there was an explosion of red.

Complete darkness.

Grant Wamack

Mr. Watts opened his eyes and yellow light flooded the room. Prisma looked down at him with joy, her face wet with tears.

"Mr. Watts, I thought you were dead. Thought I was alone . . . "

Mr. Watts managed to smile through the pain. He owed it to Prisma; after all, she brought joy to his life and was the closest thing to a familial tie.

"What are those lights?"

"What lights?" Prisma asked, looking around the room, but failed to see any light besides that belonging to Mr. Watts.

Small pinpoints of light floated around the room, growing stronger by the minute. One drifted down and settled on the dead body of the Telemarketer. It whirred and buzzed, then glowed.

Now Prisma noticed the lights too. "Fireflies."

"They're beautiful."

Something small hit the ceiling. Then it was followed by another and another until it sounded like the whole satellite was being hit by small pebbles.

"Is it raining?" Mr. Watts asked.

"That's not rain." Prisma's eyes widened.

"What is it then?"

"It's Telemarketers. Thousands of them—crawling on the roof—trying to find a way inside."

Mr. Watts looked past Prisma's face and moved his eyes upward to the huge ceiling. Black silhouettes were superimposed over the yellow windows. They moved quickly—skittering overhead—never once stopping in one place. Eventually, their numbers grew and they merged into one giant black smudge of darkness.

Mr. Watts's lightbulb began to flicker, alternating between light and dark.

Prisma was there one second and swallowed up by darkness the next. Then her worried face was lit up once again.

Prisma grabbed Mr. Watts's head and brought it inches away from her own. "Mr. Watts, *please* don't do this. Not now. Don't die. Don't fucking do this. You're all I have left."

"It's going to be okay," Mr. Watts mumbled, eyes barely open, trying his best to keep them focused on Prisma. He wanted her face to be his last memory, the last image left on his retina.

"It's not going to be okay." Prisma's voice cracked.

Through sheer determination and one last surge of energy, Mr. Watts painfully sat up, grabbed Prisma's shoulders and kissed her soft lips.

"I love you."

He began to cough and lay back down; his light flickered on and off and back on again.

Overhead, the windows were cracking, straining to contain the Telemarketers' immense weight. It was going to break any second now.

Prisma laid Mr. Watts's head on her lap and began to caress it softly. She opened her mouth, paused, and began to sing.

Her voice was beautiful, light as a feather, but powerful enough to fill the whole room. It was fresh honey, morning dew, all of these things and so much more.

Mr. Watts closed his eyes and listened to the most beautiful song caress his ears and open his heart.

Plants began to creep into the room, through cracks and vents, choking machines, straining to hear the voice reverberating throughout the satellite.

The tide was coming. Mr. Watts could hear its subtle waves underneath Prisma's soft voice.

The windows continued to break; glass tinkled down and there was a harmonious hissing.

Prisma sang the last sorrowful note, wiped a warm tear from her eye, and Mr. Watts's light went out completely.

Fade to black.

A LIGHTBULB'S LAMENT

GRANT WAMACK

About the Author

Grant Wamack is a weird fiction writer, rapper, traditional artist, urban mystic and works as a mass communication specialist for the Navy. He is the author of the bizarro novella, *Notes from the Guts of a Hippo*, and currently resides in Spain where he dances with beautiful ghosts in cobblestone streets. You can find him hiding here:
http://grantwamack.wordpress.com/

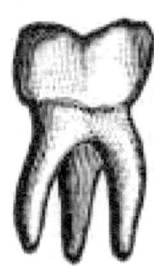

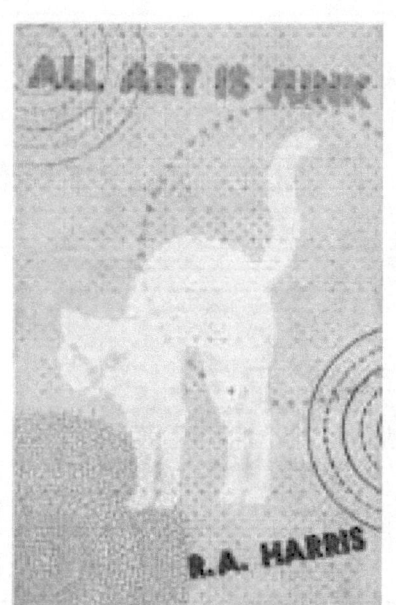

ALL ART IS JUNK

Lana Rivers, a girl with paintbrush hair, is missing and it's up to Lancelot, her cyborg knight, and his bionic conjoined twin, Cilia, to find her before her evil father, a disrespected artist turned mad-scientist, performs a terrible experiment on her.

WWW.BIZARROPULPPRESS.COM

CUCUMBER PUNK

On the fringe of an acceptable society, Pete's a cucumber-headed punk whose thoughts of rebellion against the social order frustrate him to no end. Sometimes, there's a shortage of tomato sauce. But there's no shortage of fear for the Veg-heads, as they're hunted down to satisfy the Norms and their consumer culture...

FECAL TERROR

A killer turd is on the loose!

WWW.BIZARROPULPPRESS.COM

THE AFTER-LIFE STORY OF PORK KNUCKLES MALONE

What's a farm boy to do when his pet pig becomes an evil, decaying hunk of ham with slime-spewing psychic powers?

NOTES FROM THE GUTS OF A HIPPO

A rugged journalist by the name of Jay Robbins is sent on a mission to the dangerous jungles of Brazil to search for a missing hippopotamus researcher and a news story. Along the way, he stumbles upon a mythical breed of hippo, the Lastir, which harbors another world within its guts and secrets he could only imagine. It won't be easy though. With two elderly assassins trailing him and a bunch of notes, Robbins has his job cut out for him.

WWW.BIZARROPULPPRESS.COM

THE HORROR SHOW

A Nobel Prize-winning poet has been missing for several years, along with his wife and child. Suffering from narcolepsy and amnesia, the poet wanders the same back-alleys he terrorized as a teenager. He's being carefully watched by Doctor Humphrey, whose unique treatment plan is driven by a higher power that wants a cure for mental instability to produce the ultimate war machines. At the mercy of his derangements and the ghosts of his fragmented past, the poet's descent into the darkest reaches of his soul reveals a blood-soaked past which threatens to repeat itself.

www.ingramcontent.com/pod-product-compliance
Lightning Source LLC
Chambersburg PA
CBHW020253150626
46552CB00020B/843